Nothing
in
Common

AN ANTHOLOGY
OF LOVE STORIES

Marianne Borgia

Visit our website at www.StillwaterPress.com for more information.

First Stillwater River Publications Edition

ISBN-13, 978-1-946-30063-8
ISBN-10, 1-946300-63-2

1 2 3 4 5 6 7 8 9 10

Written by Marianne Borgia
Cover design by Nathanael Vinbury

Published by Stillwater River Publications, Pawtucket, RI, USA.

Dedication

This book is dedicated to the love of my life, my late husband, Andre, who broadened my vision of life.

Table of Contents

Acknowledgements

I want to acknowledge Dr. Josephine Ruggiero,
teacher of my creative writing group,
who was the impetus for my decision to publish
and who was most helpful, along with my class members.

Nothing in Common

NOTHING IN COMMON

*S*he had never loved him. She had married him, professing love for him, but she never loved him. Yes, she was fond of him, but there was no burning passion for a newlywed like herself. After having met various men in the past, she had never fallen in love. She was beginning to give up hope.

Sara met Elliot when she had been visiting with her friend, Frances, in the nation's capital. Both girls had done the touristy things, seeing all the great monuments, etc. However, Frances also knew some politicos and had wrangled an invitation to a cocktail party. While at the party, Sara met several people.

One of the men there made a beeline in her direction. "Did I overhear that you come from Rhode Island?" he said. "Yes" she replied. "Oh, I have a home there" he said. "What do you do there?"

he continued. "Well, after I graduated college, I got a job with the State as a legal assistant to one of the legal counsels for a State agency," she said.

"Let me introduce myself. My name is Elliot. And you are?"

"I am Sara."

She quickly admitted to herself that she liked the attention this man was giving her. Was it the drink, the attention, or what that made her very talkative? "I also do calligraphy work for people who need that sort of work."

Elliot interjected with a question, "What specifically do you do with that calligraphy work?"

"Well, there are invitations, greeting cards, signs, menus. Lots of things where people like a really nice way of presenting the written word to others."

"Interesting" he smiled.

That's how it all began.

A woman as attractive as Sara, with her blond hair and blue eyes, should not have had difficulty attracting men. And she did not. But she could not find "the one". When Elliot entered her life and became enamored of her, she was elated. If she succumbed to his marriage entreaties, perhaps she would come to love him. Possibly, being in a marital relationship she would feel differently and eventually feel passion for him. Truth was that even in the throes of intercourse, she found much missing. Elliot always thought she enjoyed it, but it was all perfunctory. Yes, the body enjoys some aspects of lovemaking, but Sara generally found it was not so with Elliot. In her heart of hearts she did not love him. She did what she had to do, but there was nothing special there.

She was already tired of it all, though it had only been two years since their marriage. Elliot had asked her to give up her job, so life became luncheons for social causes, volunteer work and her calligraphy. Elliot was always proud of her. His work in Washington,

D.C. took him away from home a great deal. He worked for one of the many Congressional people. Since homes were so costly there, he roomed with two other associates. Between his work there and missions out of the country, he was rarely home. His friends thought he was a lucky man. When they met Sara, all thought his wife was beautiful and charming. None knew that Sara was not happy, nor in love. She felt the marriage had been a sham. The beautiful home and all the luxury that went with it was not fulfilling. Although Elliot provided well for her and would call her often to explain what was going on with his work, she was unhappy.

The godsend in her life was the work she had found for herself. Something she had always enjoyed enormously. Most nights she was out singing at a small club called Mel's Bells. An unusual name, but it did have a following. It was an intimate cafe in the center of town where she sang with a trio consisting of a piano, bass and drums. She loved the work which got her away from her loveless marriage. Elliot did not object. He realized she needed to do that which made her happy, since she was alone so much.

And that was how her life went. She simply did not know what to make of it nor where she was going to correct it all.

Because the club where she worked was in the center of town and near several hotels, travelers would often stop in for a drink or two and listen to some music and singing.

Sara was always polite to whomever made a request for a song. If she and the trio knew it, they would comply.

One night a man about Sara's age came in. sat down, ordered a drink and looked at her. He noticed how others made song requests and listened to Sara as she sang. She had a lush voice. Quiet applause followed.

Understanding now how it was done, he addressed his request aloud to her, "Roma Non Fa La Stupida Stasera" (Rome Do Not Be Foolish Tonight). Sara was startled at the request. He had an accent.

She actually knew the words and knew the song. The trio, however, did not.

She looked over to where he sat and simply replied "Mi dispiace" (I'm sorry). He smiled and said nothing.

Other requests were made and she went on from there. Who was that man with the unusual request? She sought him out as she perused the room after completing her set. She did not see him again.

As her time at the club finished, she prepared to go home. It was late. She was startled while opening her car door to hear a man say, "Che piacere, qualcuno che parla la mia lingua" (What a pleasure, someone who speaks my language).

She hurriedly got into her car and did not reply. It was late and she was not going to talk to a perfect stranger at this late hour and in this place. She drove away, smiling to herself.

She recognized the man with the accent when he again came into the club. He no longer made a request, but simply came into the club, had a drink, and then left.

One night, when he had again come to the club, he asked the waiter if Sara could sit with him for a drink. The waiter hesitated, knowing Sara did not usually sit with the customers. However, he passed on the information to Sara. She was intrigued by the request. For some unknown reason, she went to his table.

He stood up. Nice and tall and handsome, she thought. He offered his hand and said, "My name is Bernardo."

She replied, "I am Sara."

"Please sit down," said he. "It was a pleasure to hear someone who understood my language."

"I studied it in school," she said.

In order to make the proper introduction, he said, "I own that small restaurant not too far from here. Bettina's Restaurant."

"Oh," she said, "is that your wife's name?"

"No, no, no" he said. "That's my mother's name."

"Really?" she said, with some skepticism.

He was very polite with her, but what exactly did he want with her?

"I am always looking for new business. I hope you will visit my place some time since you are nearby. The food is simple, but good." Hurriedly, he added "I even have a new pasta machine that is quite unique. You might want to see how it works."

Where was this man going with this conversation, she thought?

"That's interesting" she said

Bernardo was hoping to make some inroads with this woman, but he did not think he was doing too well in that department. "Believe me, I am harmless. My restaurant is a very public place. Let's say, it is perfectly safe for you to come there."

For the first time, she laughed softly.

Bernardo quickly said, "You are beautiful when you relax and laugh."

"Thank you" she replied demurely.

Then Bernardo said, "How about tomorrow night, after your work here?"

Anything to get out of this situation. She thought about it for a while and then said, "Very well."

The next night as she was leaving the club, she remembered what she had told him and the arrangement she had made with him.

When she finally drove to his restaurant, she found all the lights on. When she knocked on the door, Bernardo came to greet her. "Wonderful to see you," he casually said. "Do come in."

"Where are all the patrons?" she said.

"Oh, it's the end of the day and everyone has gone."

"Come in" he said nonchalantly. "I'll show you the pasta machine." Then he reverted to Italian and said, "Ti faccio vedere come é facile a fare la pasta fresca" (I'll show you how easy it is to make fresh pasta).

As Sara sat quietly on a stool watching, Bernardo pulled a small machine from his cupboard. It was quite new, he said, and an easy way to make pasta.

He measured a cup of flour, a cup of semolina, and four eggs. He placed them all in a small container and attached it to the machine. He pushed a button and the machine began to knead those ingredients together. After a bit he pushed another button that said "extrude" and out came the pasta.

It was fettucine. At intervals, he would cut them a certain length as they came out of the machine. When all was done, he set them on a floured board. The pasta was completed in a matter of a few minutes.

He smiled at her and said, "Questa macchina é fantastico. (This machine is fantastic)."

She smiled at his enthusiasm and simply said, "Very nice."

After he had washed and dried his hands, he approached her. She did not move away. He took her hands and said in English, "Some things are so easy."

Sara knew what he was implying, but did not reply. Instead, she looked around the restaurant. "Do you do a good business?"

He realized she was changing the subject. He sat back. "In fact, I do. Noon time it gets quite busy. The food seems to satisfy everyone and I get a lot of repeats. That really makes me feel good."

Sara smiled and stood up. "Nice to hear that." She pulled on her coat and headed for the door. "You'll excuse me, Bernardo. I must go now."

Once she was out the door, Bernardo hit both hands hard on the counter, muttering a few angry words. He knew he had not made a good impression on her. A hurried conversation with her was not what he had in mind. Sara fascinated him. He wanted to see her again.'

Thereafter, when he saw her at the club, he would simply wave to her and after a drink or two, was on his way. Sara often looked for him, but many nights she did not see him.

She found herself thinking of him often—more often than she should have. What was it about this man?

* * *

Her curiosity got the better of her. One afternoon she found herself in the vicinity of his restaurant. Yes, she wanted to see him again. She did not know how to approach this. Well, as he had told her, it was a public place and she had been there before. Timidly now, she entered the restaurant. It was after the lunch hour and there were no patrons about.

When he saw her, he smiled broadly. "A cup of espresso for you, miss," he joked. She smiled back. "Fine," she said. It was daylight hours, so she assumed it was safe to be here.

Then he said seriously, "It's wonderful to see you, Sara."

"Thank you," she replied.

"I'll make us some espresso. Is that fine with you?"

She nodded and sat down at one of the tables. She looked around his restaurant while he prepared the beverage.

When all was ready, he sat opposite her.

Before he could say anything, she asked how he had come to live in America.

Bernardo sighed. "My father had a trattoria outside of Rome. I met many American tourists. I was intrigued by their attitude about everything. Most had never suffered wars and had a laisser-faire way of approaching most things. I had studied some English and was able to interact with them. I thought coming to America would be an interesting adventure. My uncle in the northeast sponsored my entry here. He helped me open this small home-style restaurant and so I got to know America and Americans first hand. I simply enjoyed their way of viewing things. My restaurant was in a good spot and I made some money. And here I am."

"What about you, Sara? You look like a woman that seems to have it all. Am I right about that?"

"Nothing unusual about me. I lead a very ordinary life. I have my evening job which I enjoy a great deal. I also do some calligraphy work. I got married a couple of years ago and live on the east side of town. My husband works in Washington, D.C. as a congressional aide and comes home now and then. That's about it," she said.

"Oh," he said. "Are you happy in your marriage?"

How impertinent of him! She looked down at the table and nodded.

He smiled and said, "I don't believe you, Sara. You are looking for something." Boldly, he continued, "Do you think you found it in me?"

Her anger showed itself instantly. Then she said, "I don't know." Suddenly she wanted to run from this spot. He took her hand across the table. She almost recoiled, but she could not. She wanted his hand on hers.

Quietly he said, "I know, my dear Sara. Whatever you are feeling, I am feeling too. That is why you are here now."

She quickly arose from her seat and said, "Bernardo, I must leave now."

"Sara," he said, "you can run, but you know as well as I what will probably happen." He kissed her hand. Sara ran from the restaurant. Bernardo continued to sit at the table. He was glum. He found himself murmuring her name.

He had to get his head on straight. Day in, day out he went about doing what he had to do, but the sight of her floated before his eyes. There were other women. Several to choose from. Sara was a married woman. What was he doing? He did not want to become embroiled in a situation of this sort. He had to forget her. Nothing to do with a married woman. Not at all.

However, Sara haunted his thoughts. Several nights later he came into the club and waved to her. He needed to get a note to her. As she moved among the patrons, he was able to slip her his note. When she finally read the note, it simply said, "I must see you tonight at my place."

Am I a glutton for punishment, she thought? She had to find out what this was all about.

When she arrived at his restaurant, he ushered her into his apartment behind the restaurant. "I did not know you had an apartment here," she said.

"It makes it much easier after a long day not to have to travel all about town for a place to rest. Please sit down." They both did.

He made small talk about his busy day. All he needed now was a drink. He offered her one, but she declined.

Then she took a deep breath and said, "What is so urgent?"

"Sara," he said seriously "I come to the club often not to hear you sing or admire your beauty. I have this great attraction to you, which I cannot understand. I know you are married, but I think of you frequently, more than I should. I would never approach a married woman, but…."

Sara gasped. Now she knew why she was here. Without compunction, she heard her heart speak aloud for her. "Yes, I am here for you."

When Bernardo heard what she said, he stood up and moved slowly towards her. Their eyes locked. He took her hand and helped her arise. Quietly, he said, "You're not leaving here tonight until I get what I've been wanting from you."

She allowed him to pull her into his arms. He caressed her cheek and kissed her gently as he held her tightly. Everything felt so good, she thought.

He could not wait any longer. Firmly, he took her by the hand to his bed. "You are simply beautiful, Sara. I've wanted you since the first night I saw you." She looked up at him. She hesitated. What was expected of her?

He saw her timidity and helped her shed her clothes. She did not resist nor did she flinch. Quickly, he removed and tossed his clothes aside. He began stroking her thigh up to her buttocks, and whispered that which excited her. Kissing virtually every part of her body, he murmured, "Your body feels like silk." A great sexual urge overcame her. She was soaring with pleasure. No one had ever done what he was doing to her. She moaned. Bernardo wanted to hear her as she completely enjoyed this intimate moment between them. He tried to move slowly, but she was as hungry for him as he was for her.

When they were finally joined, her climax was imminent. The pleasure encompassed him also when it happened. He could wait no longer and his release was spectacular. His moans matched hers. He held her close. The proximity of his body thrilled her. Such a glorious experience.

After they were completely spent, he let her go and breathlessly sighed, "Beautifully done, Sara. Beautifully done." Just what he had wanted.

Somehow, she did not know how to respond, but looked at him with her blue eyes. He began to get dressed, waiting for her to say something. She said nothing. All she did then was to look down at her hands. Those hands had touched him so lovingly and erotically.

He understood her trepidations. Tonight he had felt her need. What was she thinking? What more did she want? She did not move.

Her thinking was muddled. She should not have become involved in this way. Was it right or wrong? All she knew was that he excited her.

Because neither spoke, there was tension in the air. Finally, he went to the door and said, "I have to get some fresh air. Please let yourself out." Again, she said nothing. Without her response, he said angrily, "Possibly, another day." He was quickly out the door. She noticed he had banged the door hard.

Once dressed, she left hurriedly. Never had she felt so possessed. Driving home she thought this beautiful man had awakened something in her. Such sexual pleasure. Did she want to see him again? Oh, yes.

For several weeks after their first encounter, Bernardo thought of her. He wanted to be with her again. To him she was so desirable even though he had known many women. Sara intrigued him in a most indefinable way. She was beautiful, engaging, smart and so many things he could not enumerate. Waiting to see her again was so difficult. They had not exchanged telephone numbers, nor communicated in any way.

Finally one night he drove to the nightclub, waiting in the parking lot for her to emerge. When he saw her, he called out to her. She was startled.

"I had to see you again, Sara," he whispered. "I didn't know how to get in touch with you."

"Bernardo, I don't know what to say."

"Come to my apartment, please," he said.

"I was on my way home," she replied.

"Is anyone waiting for you at home?"

She hesitated. "No one."

He took the bull by the horns and said, "Follow me in my car." "Now," he emphasized.

She looked at him, then stopped. She moved to her car, as he had directed.

When they finally reached his apartment, he helped her out of her car. He opened his apartment door. She preceded him. She did not know what to say.

When he opened his arms to her, she went willingly. He kissed her lightly on the mouth and said "You taste good. You have no idea how you continually arouse me. All I want is you close to me." Then he added, "Don't be afraid of me. I'll never hurt you."

"I know that." She sighed "I haven't been able to get you out of my mind."

He hugged her tightly and said, "Sara, I can't get enough of you." He stopped for a moment, lifted her chin and continued kissing her, first softly and sweetly. Then there was a great urgency as their lips met. "Don't say anything. Just let me touch you everywhere and feel your beautiful body close to me."

For several moments, he held her, pulled her hair away from her face. Again there was that passion that was burning up inside of him. As he picked her up and placed her on his bed, he heard her murmur, "Please".

Bernardo stopped and looked down at her. "Is that please stop, or please continue?" Those blue eyes made him melt. With her arms around his neck, she pulled him towards her. Now he knew.

He whispered, "I want to always please you and I want you to always please me. You are so desirable and you excite me. You are…" He was looking for the right word. "You are luxurious."

The sweetness of her voice was intoxicating to him. "I don't know what else you want me to say. I am here for you."

"By now you know there is no woman I want more than you. Let me enjoy all the excitement—every bit of it," he said.

Whatever ecstasy was, the evening proved ecstatic for both of them. She responded eagerly to him and he could not have been more satisfied nor happier with her.

Finally, he said, "I don't know what's happening here, but I must see you again." He sighed, held her tightly, and whispered, "Please come back often."

She gently touched his cheek. He took the inside of her hand and kissed it. In the most tender way, she said, "I did not know how wonderful it could be between us." At evening's end, she dressed and ran out the door. She was drunk with pleasure.

* * *

Bernardo was cleaning up in the back room of his restaurant late one night with only the light in the kitchen. Suddenly he heard banging on his front door. He was startled. When he went to answer, there stood Sara.

"What are you doing here at this hour?" he said.

The usual docile Sara was angry. "We have to talk," she said, raising her voice. He stepped aside and let her in.

When she stormed into the kitchen she began, "What am I going to do? You've become an obsession. I can hardly function. I see you in front of me constantly."

Bernardo decided he would say nothing. He let her rant on about what had transpired between them, her desire for him, and the futility of other aspects of their lives. On and on she went.

"I am so angry," she shouted.

Bernardo smiled, "You're not angry. You are in arousal and I like that."

"No, no, no," she said loudly.

He got closer. "Say no once more." He pulled her close and began to kiss her. Over and over he caressed her.

She was breathless now.

His arms were still around her. "Say no again" he insisted.

She began to murmur softly, "No. Please don't touch me."

"Stop it," he shouted. "You know you want me to touch you—over and over. You want me as much as I want you."

He stood back. He needed to maintain his composure. "Sara, any man in his right mind would take advantage of you."

Finally, holding her at bay, he turned away from her. Then once more he turned to face her, "Right now you're like a tiger, so I'm here to soothe the tiger. If I've become an obsession with you, we can remedy that."

She looked at him quizzically.

He continued, "At night why don't you come to my apartment after your work at the club."

"I don't understand."

Speaking at an even level, he continued, "Of course, you do. Maybe you can get rid of your obsession. After a little time with me, you'll see how absurd it all is."

"Is this a joke or something?"

"Dear Sara, you know by now not only am I serious, but I have an ulterior motive. Why don't you go home and think about it."

Sara did not know what to make of his suggestion.

He opened the door to let her out. He almost stopped her. Even in her agitated state, he wanted her. Instead, he finally closed the door behind her.

Looking upward, Bernardo stood alone and quietly with his back to the door. Sara did not know that while standing there, he said aloud, "Sara, you are my obsession."

For days and days thereafter, Bernardo had Sara on his mind. He had tasted her and he wanted to be with her as often as possible. Her husband came home rarely, but he did not care. Wanting her was interminable.

For days and days thereafter, Sara thought of him. He thrilled her. His touch was what she wanted. The feel of him lingered on her body. He showed her how sensual she could be and she wanted him all the more. She did not know how long she could wait to see him again.

One afternoon she called him at his restaurant. "Bernardo, can I see you at the apartment tonight?" He was surprised at her call. "Yes, by all means." He hesitated. "Sorry, I can't talk. I'm quite busy right now. See you later."

That evening as he finally held her, he stroked her arms. Then he moved to her hips. She always shivered at his touch. "God, I want you so much, Sara." His hungry kisses brought her to the brink. All he heard was "Yes, yes, yes." Now they knew what would ensue. It became unbridled passion.

She then began to meet with him at his apartment most evenings after her work at the nightclub. Ordinarily, she would have returned to an empty house. He brought appetizers and wine into his apartment from his restaurant so he could share his day with her and she with him.

Oftentimes, when she arrived, there would follow a repartee between them.

"I've been waiting for you," he said.

"I hurried," she replied.

"I count every minute until you get here," he continued.

"I can't get here fast enough," she sighed.

"Where have you been all my life?" he queried.

"I've been waiting forever for you too," she smiled.

Any excuse was the best excuse to be together, even for a few hours. They laughed and chatted about many things—their past lives and what was occurring presently. Sometimes, they would sit next to each other and watch television. They would even exchange anecdotes. On other occasions, while sitting close to him, Sara would look as he worked on his laptop going over inventory and other business matters. He would stop now and again to kiss her. "You are so delicious," he would say. Sara was so happy.

Where once she had been timid with him, now Sara found herself becoming comfortable as they spent time together. All else was a prelude to their wanting each other. Those nights together always were exquisite. Sara would return home to an empty bed, alone, but happy.

When she left him at night, nothing was said. He knew she awaited a call from Washington most mornings. He would simply say, "Drive carefully."

When Sara arrived one particular night, she hurried to Bernardo's side. He smiled, held her for a moment, and then kissed her lightly. So unlike his usual greeting. Sara looked up at him. "Bernardo, is something the matter? Did you have a bad day?" He shook his head. "Well," she continued, "what is wrong?"

Finally, he sat her on the sofa by his side and held her hands. "Sara, you are a distraction to me. A beautiful distraction."

Sara raised her eyebrows. "I don't understand. I'm here with you often."

He now placed his hands on her shoulders, shook her and blurted out "Do you see what has happened here? I've fallen madly in love with you. You're in my head and heart every single day." He shook his head "I've fallen in love with a married woman." Again, he shook his head "It's truly a dilemma." His eyes sought hers pleadingly.

He awaited her reply. Her voice was very low. "Thank you for loving me, Bernardo." That is all she said. He had wanted much more, but he had to be content with that. For now, at least.

Early one day Bernardo called Sara. "How about some drinks and dancing tonight? I know a nice spot not too far out of town. Just to get away from meeting at my apartment. What do you think?" Sara quickly agreed.

"About 10 p.m. After your show. Tomorrow is my day off. And you?"

"I have nothing tomorrow either. There's only the evening show."

Just before 10 p.m. she was at his door. Bernardo smiled at her. "You look beautiful." He kissed her lightly on the mouth. He looked at her again. She wore black silk slacks and a white silk blouse with little straps to hold it up.

"Let's go," he said. "Leave your car here."

It took them more than a half hour to find the place he had chosen. They sat down and he ordered margaritas for both of them. When they got up to dance, he held her tightly. She smiled as they danced.

"Is there something wrong?" he asked.

"I love the way you hold me." she said.

"Any which way is what I do best." He twirled her around. "You certainly know that." His hand moved up and down her spine making her tingle.

"You're making me tingle," she added.

"Hold that thought. I'll do better later," he smiled slyly.

When they were seated, he asked how she had come to sing at the club. She told him she had often been told she had a good voice. She had done a regional show for a friend at one time. All the musicians there had praised her for her voice. One encouraged her to take a few lessons. Then a friend introduced her to the owner of the small club where she now worked.

"That's how it all started," she said.

"And you?" she inquired.

He told her how he sometimes yearned to return to his native country, but there was no one to take over his business so that he could take an extended vacation. Although, he insisted, he really needed some time off.

They talked and laughed and danced again until the small hours of the morning. It was getting late, so they finally returned to his apartment since her car was there.

Bernardo asked her to come in for a minute. Once in the door, he took off his shirt.

"Sara, you have never stayed overnight. I want you to stay here tonight."

"No, I can't," she said. "I have things to do."

"But you told me you had nothing to do until the night show."

"I don't think so—not tonight" she argued

He was facing her, only about one foot away. His hands reached up to her blouse's straps. He pulled them down her arms. She was exposed from the waist up. Looking at her nakedness, he whispered, "Beautiful, absolutely beautiful." She felt awkward and was at a loss for words. His eyes were caressing her from her face to her waist.

He picked her up in his arms as one would a child, with one arm around her waist and the other supporting her legs, holding her close to his bare chest. Her arms went around his neck. She put her head down and nestled there.

"You're what I want," he murmured into her ear. "Don't expect to get much sleep tonight."

After he slowly removed her outer clothing, he noticed the only undergarment she wore were black lace-like panties. He stopped and smiled slightly. When his hands felt them, she stirred. Bernardo growled.

Her blue eyes quietly stared at him. Sara placed her arms around his shoulders. Bernardo thought how beautiful she was. As their ardor grew fiercer, he could barely feel the pain of her nails as they dug into his shoulders. There was just the intense pleasure that filled him as their bodies locked together.

In his bed she waited for him to say something. He said absolutely nothing. He began to touch her in many places. Her body shivered at each touch. His kisses became possessive and hungry. The touch of body to body was intoxicating. Now and again, he heard her murmur her pleasure. She put her hands on his chest and moved them downward very slowly. He began to breathe more heavily.

Sara had become the seductive woman he had dreamed of. Her inhibitions, with him, had fallen away. Now and then she would also initiate their lovemaking. Bernardo shook his head happily when that happened. With Sara, he could not have asked for more.

Not one word passed between them at that moment. It was like a pantomime of sexual exploration for both of them. Soon his groans would not stop and she was like a tiger waiting to be uncaged. It seemed as if they were discovering each other for the first time. The pace became more rapid as their eagerness for each other began to take root inside their bodies.

She would be there for the entire night and his desire for her intensified. He knew by her actions she too did not want anything to stop. All caution was now thrown to the wind.

* * *

When Elliot called to say he would be returning from Washington, D.C. for a day or so in conjunction with a political affair at the local opera house, Sara readied herself.

There were many people at the affair. Sara chatted amiably with the several people she knew. Her eyes surveyed the room. Unbelievably, she saw Bernardo at one end of the hall with his arm around a lovely woman, talking to another couple. Sara did not know the woman, but she almost lost her breath looking at him. As he moved about, he stopped short when he saw her. She looked gorgeous in her pink gown. Looking wordlessly at each other briefly, their eyes said much. Instead, he simply smiled, and nodded in acknowledgment.

What was he doing here, thought Sara? A disaster. When they all moved to their seats, she lost sight of him for the rest of the evening.

The next day she used a ruse to call him. "Do you have a few minutes?" she said. "Certainly" said he. "You know how to get here."

When she arrived at his apartment, he smiled. "Looking for an explanation? By the way, was that your husband?"

"Yes" she replied to both questions.

He was sitting in a chair in a straddled fashion. He waited to hear what she had to say. Instead, he began, "I am a local business man and I had an invitation to that political affair also."

She digressed. "Saw you there with some girl."

"Yes," he said. "Great girl." Sara felt uncomfortable. "I need a social life too, don't you agree?" he continued.

She nodded.

"Here's the story. I like a lady on my arm and in my life. Since you are unavailable whenever I want you socially, well..."

"But you keep telling me that you always want me," she said.

"That's absolutely true. But I'm not at your beck and call. I need to enjoy what everyone else enjoys, a nice social life, good food, fun with others, and a great sex life."

Sara stopped at his declaration. Reluctantly, she quietly continued, "Did you sleep with her?"

"My dear Sara, it's really none of your business. If you loved me as I love you, perhaps I would explain."

"But...but when we're together, we both agree it's always so wonderful."

He sighed loudly. "It's all one-sided. I happen to love you."

"But, Bernardo, you know how much I enjoy being with you." She too sighed. "It's always magic between us."

"Wake up, Sara, you know how I feel. For you it's just fun and games."

She raised her voice and stared at him intently. "No, no it's not."

"Look, I need you to love me exclusively and without reservation. You have to make a choice. I want to do with a woman everything I have done with you. I want the pleasure of it all. When you are alone at night, I want you to think what I'm planning to do with other women."

She saw his anger rising, but she placed her hands over her ears. "I don't want to hear that" she cried.

The consternation between them was hard to contain. More than ever he wanted to hold her and make her understand. Reluctantly, he restrained himself.

"Sara don't make this more difficult for me. Please."

"Bernardo don't torment me."

Now Bernardo was angry. He arose from his chair and quickly strode towards her. He grasped her by the shoulders and shook her. "Listen, Miss High Society, you have no idea what it is like to love someone and not be loved in return. That's torment."

Again heading for his chair, he turned and stared at her. He thought she looked like a chastened child. She began to walk away and prepared to leave.

He quickly grabbed her by the arm, "Remember whatever happens—and I mean this—you'll always be mine. Call it fate or destiny or whatever, but if you are close or far, or even if I never see you again, in some fashion, you will always be haunted by what happened between us. You will never again enjoy all the pleasure that was ours."

Sara ran from the room and out the door sobbing.

When he walked away from her, he was still angry. He knew he would eventually relent. He could not let her go.

Many days later, he called her. "Sara, I'm sorry about what happened when we last met. You know how I feel about you." He did not know how to phrase how he was feeling. "You know, certain situations make me angry. I want to see you as soon as possible."

On the other end of the phone, Sara hastily said, "I'll be there. Yes, yes."

While her husband led a life that took him to many far-flung destinations, she knew that soon she would be back in Bernardo's arms.

* * *

As was often the case, Bernardo would nightly be in his apartment working on his laptop, waiting for Sara. When he heard the key turn in the door lock, he smiled. His beautiful Sara had arrived. He turned around in his chair and waited for her greeting.

The door opened slowly and, with her head tilted, she peeked in at him. He, in turn, gestured at her in the same way, peeking back at her. When she came in, she removed her coat and hung it on the door hook. She turned to him and simply said "Hello."

Bernardo looked at her intently. "My God, I think of you all day and wait for you all night and all you can say is 'hello'."

She smiled and moved toward him. He grabbed her arms. "You take my breath away" he moaned. As he pulled her onto his lap, her hands went to his face and she kissed him passionately. As he tried to say something, she took his lower lip and nibbled on it. She then moved further down to his neck and again kissed him. She undid his shirt and ran her lips over his bare chest.

He was breathing heavily. She continued the kissing.

He was finally able to gasp, "This hello is really arousing me. You know that? What am I going to do with you?"

She looked at him and closed her eyes. When she opened them again, he looked into her beautiful and limpid blue eyes.

Meekly, she replied, "I happen to love you."

Taken aback, for a moment he could not believe what he heard her say. Those were the precious words he had been waiting to hear. He hugged her tightly. He softly and simply whispered, "Don't ever leave me."

Returning home later, she lay in bed hugging her pillow. She loved him.

* * *

Bernardo had often inquired about Sara's calligraphy work. Finally, he asked her if she would come by some day and do some calligraphy work for him at the restaurant. "Maybe you can do some menus for me" he said. She agreed.

"However," he admonished her, "we have to act very professional when we are in my restaurant. Even on my day off service people are coming and going."

When she came in one morning with all her calligraphic implements, he greeted her in a business-like way and showed her to a booth where she could work without disturbance. He had told her what he needed. Seeing her, he smiled and whispered "Beautiful." She went on with her assignment, while he worked in the back room, coming out occasionally to check on her.

The front door then opened. It was Mark, the postman.

"Hi, Bernardo, here we go with more mail." He then turned and saw Sara with her head down working.

"Bernardo, who is that lovely girl?"

"Oh" he said casually, "She's doing some calligraphy work for me."

"Aren't you going to introduce me?"

Bernardo did not expect that from Mark. He walked him over to Sara, "Oh, Sara, I'd like you to meet my postman, Mark."

23

"Nice to meet you, Mark" she smiled. "How are you?" She shook his hand.

"Just fine. Do you come here often? I'm here most days and I've never seen you before."

"Actually, this is a one-day job, or maybe two. But to answer your question, no I do not."

"Well," he said smiling, "I hope I'll see you here again. You bring some class to this place."

"What a nice thing for you to say" Sara replied.

Bernardo steered him to the door.

Mark said, "Aren't you interested in her?"

Bernardo, with tongue in cheek, said, "She's not my type, Mark."

"Boy, you must be blind" said Mark as he went to the exit. "If you're not interested, maybe next time I come by and she is here, I'll ask her out."

Bernardo arched his eyebrows, "Well, do as you like." As they edged towards the door, Bernardo said, "Have a good day." Hurriedly, the door was shut hard.

Sara looked at him. She could read him now. "Is something wrong?"

When he was out the door, Bernardo turned to her "What's all this nicey nicey?"

"I like to be polite to people I meet."

"He's planning on asking you out." Hastily, he continued, "By the way, hope you can finish today, just so you two won't meet again."

He turned and headed for his kitchen.

Sara called after him. He turned to her. She said, "If there weren't so many windows and so many people going by, I'd come over to reassure you."

His retort, "Can you reassure me later tonight?" Smiling, he walked away.

Although they saw each other often, it was only in his apartment. One night he made a suggestion to Sara.

"Sweetheart, what are the chances of our going away together for a few days? I know a resort a couple of hours from here where we could swim, relax, and perhaps have a good time. Mondays my restaurant is closed and I could also close down for the weekend. Besides, no one would know us if we traveled some distance from here."

The suggestion caused Sara to become enthusiastic. "I like that idea."

"We could spend some time outdoors for a change away from prying eyes."

"Can you get away?"

"Yes, yes, yes," she smiled.

He smiled back at her and kissed her lightly. "I'll make the arrangements."

The following weekend all was set in order. She left her car at his back door and climbed into his car with her small piece of luggage.

As they drove away, they were like any two people anxious for a respite.

They had started early, so en route they stopped for breakfast. They talked about a myriad of things. He looked at her and thought how lucky he was.

The resort he had chosen was a lovely spot by the sea. Sara's eyes lit up and she noted, "Very nice."

When they were finally ensconced in their room at the resort, he suggested a swim. "Do you swim?" he asked.

"Oh, I'm not the best, but I manage" she said.

She changed in the bathroom, while he changed into his swim trunks in the room. With a cover-up over her suit, they went down to the nearby beach. The hotel provided them with towels and lotions.

When they had chosen a spot, she removed her cover-up. Bernardo gaped at her. She stood in front of him in a yellow bikini.

He half smiled and said, "You must be kidding. There isn't much there. What do I do now?"

"Swim" she said. "Just swim. That will cool you off." And swim they did. When out of the water she began to rub herself with sun lotion. "I'll do that" he said. He began to coat her exposed parts with lotion. "That sure feels good" he murmured. "You don't know what I'm thinking now. It's a good thing we're not in our hotel room. You drive me crazy."

"I like driving you crazy" she laughed.

They continued to sunbath until almost lunch time.

"Sara, there is a lobster shack down the road. Do you want to lunch there?"

She nodded.

After they returned to their room and dressed for their walk to the lobster shack, he said, "There's a price to pay for that yellow bikini, you know."

"You wouldn't take advantage of me, would you?"

"Think about it. Now let's go eat."

When they walked down the street for lunch, he placed his arm around her shoulder, while she placed her arm around his waist. "You know" he said seriously "we've never been able to do this before." He looked at her "It means a great deal to me to touch you in public. I want the world to know that you belong to me."

"I know" she said. "I know." She placed her head against his chest. She continued lightly "Let's just have lunch for now."

They sat at the little restaurant. He ordered for them both. It was beer and lobster. When she had difficulty with the lobster claws, he took them from her and cracked them for her to enjoy.

When they had finished their meal, she said, "Darling, there are some shops down the street from here. Can we do some shopping?"

"Of course" said he. "Now, sweetheart, while you shop, I'll walk about here. I'll meet you over by that bench in about an hour. Is that O.K.?"

"Fine" she said. Off she went to do what all women liked to do. Shop.

In the meantime, he found a small jewelry shop. When he went in he asked to see some pendants. One he particularly liked was heart-shaped made of little white pearls on a chain. He had it boxed, wrapped, and put it in his pocket.

He thought how at peace he was here with his Sara and away from any problems. Oh, how he hoped this entire situation could be resolved soon.

When he met her an hour later she was laden with packages. He exclaimed, "Wow, we really did some shopping."

"Darling, there were so many sales" she said excitedly.

"Sweetheart, there's a sale every day" he countered. "Here let me help you." He took some of her packages with one hand and held her other hand tightly. Then he added, "We better get back so I can arrange for dinner at the hotel tonight." They walked briskly and laughed as they hurried back.

In their hotel room she was eager to show him what she had purchased. Finally, she opened a larger box and said "I got this for you. It's a cashmere sweater in a blue color."

He went over to her, pulled her to him and said, "Thank you so much. It's very attractive. Love the thought and love you."

"Now" he said, "I have something for you." When he gave her the small jewelry box and she opened it, she did not know what to say. Softly she looked at him and said, "It's so beautiful." Then she began to cry.

"Now, Sara, this was something to make you happy. Stop crying."

She melted in his arms and held onto to him "Thank you for loving me."

"Don't you want to try it on?"

"Oh, yes."

He placed it around her neck and she fingered it. "I'm going to leave it on."

Bernardo laughed. "Sara, I don't think it goes well with shorts and a T-shirt."

"I'll wear it for supper."

"Look, as soon as I get dressed, I'll go down and get us a table. Does that satisfy you? When you're ready, I'll meet you in the dining room."

The dining room was not heavily crowded, so he was able to secure a nice table for both of them.

When she finally walked into the dining room, most diners stopped to stare at her. He could not believe his eyes. She looked stunning. She wore a simple blue dress with little straps. The blue color matched her eyes. Her blond hair flowed over both her shoulders. Small diamond earrings glistened on her ears. When she finally arrived at their table, he simply said, "You look absolutely beautiful." Then he added, "I think practically every guy in this room was salivating." She smiled and fondled the pendant he had given her earlier.

After a delicious dinner with wine, he suggested the small night club also in the hotel for some drinks and dancing.

As they were walking out of the dining room, an elderly gentleman approached them "I must compliment the gentleman on having such a beautiful lady on his arm. You look very happy."

Bernardo quickly replied, "Thank you for the compliment. Yes, indeed, we are very happy."

The man walked on, turned around and waved to them.

He turned to Sara, "Wasn't that nice, sweetheart?"

Sara said, "Did you notice his wife is the lady in the wheelchair?"

"No" he said.

As they continued on their way, he once again put his arm around her shoulder. "Love you, sweetheart." She hugged him.

There was a nice little combo in the night club. After being directed to a table, Bernardo ordered drinks for both of them. He stood up and took her hand. "Would you like to dance?" he said.

"Of course."

Bernardo was a very good dancer. She looked at him and said, "I didn't know you were such a good dancer."

He looked at her and said, "I learned long ago what ladies like and I tried to be a decent dancer and keep the ladies happy.".

"You certainly know how to keep this lady happy."

"I'm doing my best with you, beautiful."

When they sat down, the same elderly gentleman again approached them.

"Excuse me, my name is George and my wife at the other table is Ann. Could I make an unusual request? My wife cannot dance. Could I have one dance with your lovely lady?"

Before Bernardo could reply, Sara got up and said, "I'd love that."

She took George's hand and stepped onto the dance floor with him.

Bernardo got up and went to where Ann was sitting in her wheel chair.

"Well, they make a nice-looking couple, don't they?" Then he hesitated and said, "I'm Bernardo and that's my Sara."

"I agree with my husband. You look so happy. Are you married?"

Bernardo thought fast, "Not yet, but not too far in the future, I hope."

"Well, I hope you'll be as happy as George and I have been. We've been married 55 years. Frankly, even with a few bumps in the road of life, we've had a very good life together. I hope the same for you and Sara."

"What a nice thing for you to say, Ann." He took her hand and kissed it. He turned to the dance floor and said, "I think Fred and Ginger out there have finished their dance."

As Sara and George left the dance floor smiling, George said to Bernardo, "Your Sara is lovely, but Ann is my most beautiful woman." He turned to them both saying, "Thanks for the dance." He returned to his table and his Ann.

Holding hands and walking away, Bernardo turned to Sara and said, "If you made George happy for a few minutes, imagine how happy you make me." He hugged her tightly. Sara's eyes sparkled. She quickly kissed him on the cheek.

Though they resumed their dancing, they said very little but simply held on to each other.

When they returned to their hotel room, they were both thinking about what the elderly couple had said. "Something to look forward to, isn't it." Quietly, she agreed.

To lighten the mood, he turned to Sara, "About that yellow bikini..."

"Oh, no, you don't," she said. Then she began tickling him, knowing he had a few ticklish spots. "Sara, stop that!" Sara laughed, but continued. He pinned her arms down to the bed. Rather than being angry, he bent down to kiss her. Each kiss got deeper. He let go of her hands. Instead she placed her arms around his neck and whispered, "You're incredible."

Slowly, he took his finger, running it along her upper lip and then along her lower lip. She sweetly bit it. He smiled. "When did you become so sexy?" "Knowing you like this" she replied seductively as she caressed him. He held her tighter, "You know I like sexy and you do wonderful things to me. You're what I've always wanted." Hurriedly, they tossed their clothes to the floor. "No more talking. I just want your soft, silky body next to me" he sighed. As the moon rose high in the sky, the night was theirs alone. Their senses demanded a night for love.

The next morning was spent simply swimming and lolling in the sun.

"Do you know what our plans are for the rest of the day, sweetheart?"

She shook her head.

"There's a schooner nearby that cruises at sundown. Then it's dinner."

"Sounds wonderful." Her lips sweetly touched his. "You think of everything."

Since there was time before the dinner cruise, they took a long walk by the sea. Now was the time to enjoy being together. Time was short.

"Let's hurry and go change our clothes for our evening cruise," he said.

When the sun was lower in the sky, they boarded the schooner for a cruise and later for dinner. They were casually dressed.

Sara was so animated. She engaged perfect strangers in conversations and always looked so interested in whatever they talked to her about. From the people who worked on board or the many other guests, she gave them her complete attention.

Bernardo had never seen her like this and he enjoyed every moment as he saw her so happy. To himself he thought how wonderful their lives would be without the encumbrances that faced them. He wanted life to be like this forever. He loved her and unfortunately nothing was perfect in their lives. Not to think of that now. Not now.

After dinner and as the sun set, they stood by the ship's railing.

"Darling," she said, "please hug me."

"Sara are you cold?"

"No" she replied. "Just hold me." He held her tightly.

He didn't have to ask, but he did. "Are you happy being with me, Sara?"

"Oh, darling" she reassured him. "You know I am. Very much so."

The ship continued to cruise along the tranquil waters. Bernardo turned to her, "I remember the first time I saw you at the club. An arrow went through my heart. I probably did a lot of foolish things at the start, but I just knew I had to know you better and be with you. I love you, my dearest Sara."

Soon this brief and happy time together would end and they would be living their furtive lives again.

* * *

Bernardo was completely mystified. Sara had not been in touch with him for several days. He was concerned. There was no reply when her cell phone rang. He left no messages. She knew his number. What had happened? It was so unlike her not to answer his calls.

Finally a couple of days later he recognized her number when his cell phone rang. He hurried to answer it. Sara was sobbing.

"Sara, what's happened?"

"He's home" he heard her muffled cry.

"Oh...I see." He paused for a moment. "What can I say? What do you want me to do?" There were so many questions, but whatever answers she gave him were not the ones he wanted to hear.

Between sobs, she continued, "He wants us to go away for a while."

"What did you say?"

"I don't want to... not at all. Not now. I cannot leave here."

Bernardo sighed and softly said, "Neither do I want you to."

What a dilemma. Her husband could ask anything of her, but Bernardo could not. It was heartbreaking for him—and probably for Sara too.

"Sara, I'm usually not at a loss for words, but I don't know what to say."

Sara pleaded, "Pick me up after the show tonight. Please. I want to see you."

"O.K." he sighed.

That night he hurried to the club's parking lot and waited for her to exit. When he saw her, he started to move in her direction, but there was a man beside her with his hand on her shoulder saying, "Sara, you were great. A little somber, but good." He hugged her.

Bernardo stopped in his tracks and did a quick turnaround as if looking for his car.

It was her husband. Bernardo climbed into his car and drove away without looking back to see if she had noticed him or not.

For the first time ever, he was stymied. He absolutely did not know what to do.

When he returned to his apartment, he sat down, turned on the television, and simply continued to stare at it. He had turned it on just to hear voices to take away the dullness in his heart.

Sara, in the meantime, had seen him. She froze for a moment as Bernardo turned towards her. He had not immediately noticed that she was not alone. She did not want him to confront her and her husband, as her eyes would give her away. Her heart ached.

When she and Elliot drove away, she said little, excusing herself by saying she was tired.

Elliot was understanding, as he stroked her leg.

In her head she was screaming "No, not tonight." She had few choices. Elliot had not been home in some time and had not seen her. Yes, he provided her with a beautiful home and all the amenities. She no longer wanted them. She only wanted that man she had seen so frequently now and made her feel so wonderful.

In bed when Elliot took her in his arms, she knew his lovemaking would be hasty. He was one of those men who hurriedly took care of his own needs. He did not know or understand what it was like to be sensual or to have a woman feel sensual. She closed her eyes. When he was done with her, she turned with her back to him and silently cried.

The next morning at breakfast, Sara decided to maintain her composure.

"Elliot" she said "Why do we have to go away? You do so much traveling around the world in your job. Don't you want to stay here and discover your own home city. Besides, you said you would only be here a few days."

Elliot mulled her words over and replied, "Hmm. You are probably right. We could do some things together around town."

Sara quickly interjected by saying, "Remember I also have my calligraphy work and my volunteer work at the library."

"I suppose I could relax here at home. I repeat, we could do some things together."

"That sounds like the better solution," she replied.

When Elliot left the house, she called Bernardo on her cell phone. She had to talk to him. He might be able to allay many of her concerns and her unhappiness.

"Where and when can we meet?" she urged him.

"Are you sure we should meet?" he said.

"Please, please," she insisted.

"How about the Siesta Motel. Drive to the back of the motel where no one can see us" he said. "I'll be there at 2 p.m."

At 2 p.m. she was there. Parking behind the motel was an unobtrusive way to meet.

He was already in the room he had chosen. When she rushed into his arms, he hugged her tightly and simply kissed her on the forehead.

"Sara" he admonished her, "do not cry."

Quickly she told him the trip was off. She had talked Elliot into staying home.

Bernardo was in a quandary. "Sara, we can't go on like this."

"But, darling, he's only home for a few days."

"Don't you understand" he said angrily "I don't like this situation at all. We spend all our time together in my apartment. I love you, but I can't take you anywhere. I'm just an appendage in your life. I have my pride. I don't know if loving you is right or wrong, but remember it has never been tawdry."

Then she was stunned by what he said next.

"Obviously, staying with your husband is the better choice."

With his hand on the door, he decided to end the conversation. "Remember, I truly love you. This situation is agony for me." Then he continued, "Don't you understand?"

Before she could say more, he was quickly out the door.

The situation was becoming untenable. When her husband came home, usually it was only for a few days, but for Bernardo it seemed like forever. There was no finality to matters. He was in limbo. After work at his restaurant, he would sometimes go and play soccer with his friends. Other times he would get together with those same friends at a bar for a few drinks and some raucous guy stories. However, when he climbed into bed, he missed Sara most of all. He would dream of the silky smoothness of her body next to him. His mind ran rampant over so many scenarios. He could have dated, as he still had a few lady friends. Often, he did not.

Why Sara? Many women would have given him all the time and loving he wanted. Sara. A married woman, no less. What irony! The lady friends from the nearby hospital who frequented his restaurant would joke about whom among them he would take out. He made light of it all. He did not want to lose them as customers. He had even heard one of them whisper that he might be gay. Was this what he was reduced to? A virile, sensuous man like him.

The more he thought about it, the more he realized that he had to get away for a while. Having made his decision, he told Sam, his assistant cook, his plans and asked him to take over matters at the restaurant. Sam agreed to keeping things in order while Bernardo was away. However, Bernardo asked him not to inform others about his whereabouts. He did not tell Sara his plans.

Once gone, Sara sought him. When she went to his apartment, she found it closed. Although she still had a key, her endless visits there were fruitless.

She went to his restaurant looking for him and seeking some information. She told Sam that Bernardo had asked her to do some calligraphy work for him. What else could she say? Sam shrugged his shoulders and told her he had no information about Bernardo. Simply, he had gone away.

Not knowing of Bernardo's whereabouts, Sara barely functioned each day. As Elliot's wife she continued to be invited to luncheons for social causes. Also, there was her calligraphy work and her volunteer work at the local library. But, she was heartbroken and no longer knew what to do.

* * *

Bernardo was quite tired after his long overseas flight home. He had been away a few weeks. After paying the taxi driver, he picked up his luggage, and sought the key to his restaurant. When he turned the lock to the darkened restaurant, he placed his luggage on the floor and yawned. Everything seemed to be in order, although he noticed there was a sliver of light in his adjacent apartment. Who or what was that? He opened the apartment door and hurried in. Unbelievably, he saw Sara asleep on his couch. His heart skipped a beat. What was she doing here?

He approached her and softly called her by name. When she slowly opened her eyes and saw him, she jumped up and her arms quickly pulled him to her.

"Where have you been?" Louder, she repeated, "Where have you been?"

He took her in his arms and simply cried out her name repeatedly. "What are you doing here?"

"I still have the key. I come most nights hoping you would return." She placed her arms around his neck and kissed him several times.

"I don't understand" he said.

"I knew you had to return sooner or later."

He continued, "I can't believe this. After all these weeks the one I want to see is here before me."

They began to talk over each other. After an interminable time, he finally stopped and smiled. "Okay, you first."

"Tell me where you've been?" she queried.

"Well" he said, "I had to get away for a bit and think what I needed to do about you."

"But...." she started to say.

"Sweetheart," he interrupted, "I had to straighten out things in my head. I had to see if being away would help me forget you.

Despite where I went, I kept seeing you." He sighed. "I can't let you go. I love you too much."

She quickly replied, "But don't you remember when I told you I loved you, you said 'Don't ever leave me'. Yet you went off and left me here without a word or explanation." Her eyes were teary.

He looked down and nodded, mumbling "I'm so sorry, Sara."

She continued. "You've said over and over that you love me. Here I was not knowing what to do."

He hugged her. "I'm truly sorry for that, Sara. Please, please forgive me. I didn't know where we two were going or what would happen next between us. I was so mixed up."

She said nothing, but placed her arms around his waist and laid her head on his chest.

He caressed and kissed her repeatedly. It was his peace offering.

"I have a lot to tell you, but I am quite tired after that long flight. I desperately need sleep." Then he cupped his hand under her chin. "Please sleep with me tonight."

"Yes, yes" she said eagerly. "We need to talk."

When they finally went to bed, he promptly fell asleep. She lay next to him for some time thinking about what had ensued. His body next to her was what she had been waiting for. Then she too fell asleep.

The following morning when she opened her eyes, he was looking at her. "Are you awake, sweetheart?"

When she smiled, he whispered "I didn't come back just to look at you." He moved towards her. "Don't hurry me, even if it's been a long time between us. Understand?" He looked at her in a steady fashion, while he got closer still. "I want everything to last." Again, he said, "Understand?"

In a hushed voice, she replied, "Don't tease me."

"I won't" he answered.

She waited for his kiss. Instead, he grasped her hips and his mouth sweetly moved down her stomach. Sara shivered with delight. Then as he continued, she cried out his name. Her head turned involuntarily from side to side as her body began to respond to him. Once more, there was the wonderful thrill of him. When he whispered erotic words to her, she complied. The arousal was great for both of them and continued for some time.

Long afterwards, sated and breathless, they lay side by side wordlessly. Sara finally asked him about his trip.

Bernardo told her he had visited London, Paris, and the south of France. He had rented a car and simply roamed from place to place.

Sara asked if he had met any people in his travels. He said yes. He had met a couple of women whom he had taken out to dinner. "I know what you are going to ask me. No, I did not sleep with either of them. I simply took each of them to dinner. I needed someone to talk to now and again." He hesitated. "I would not lie to you, sweetheart."

She gazed at him. "A sexy man like you, Bernardo, only talked. Really?"

He gripped her arms. "Look at me. You're the only woman I want."

Her eyes were downcast.

As he arose from the bed, he turned to her and said, "Now, I'm going to take a shower."

Sara looked at him. He was the sort of man any woman would want.

He startled her by picking her up from the bed. He was headed for the shower. Once there, he moved her up against the tile wall and looked at her so lovingly.

"What do you think we are going to do now?" Before she could answer, he turned on the warm water. It cascaded over them.

"I'm not going to shower alone. I have not seen or touched you in a long time. We both need more loving. In fact, lots of loving." His hands were all over her.

Happily ensconced in the shower and with the water raining down on them, she now placed her arms around his neck. They were once again whetting their sexual appetite. There was nothing else to say.

* * *

Their lives resumed as before. Bernardo was still the lover he had always been. Sara was always happy to be with him. Phone calls from Elliot came once in a while. He seemingly was always busy with his work in Washington or his frequent travel overseas. Elliot kept her up to date on what he was doing, but Sara thought he was so involved in his work that as his wife she was only something he could brag about. He could always tell those he knew that he had a considerate and loving wife back home who understood his devotion to his work. But he rarely visited home. Before they married, his life had been somewhat like that of a vagabond. Even now, as a married man, it continued in that fashion. Sara had learned long ago not to expect him home frequently. She went on with her solitary life. Bernardo was her saving grace.

Although, the fact was that with his return, even Bernardo seemed somewhat remote on occasion. She could not fathom what it was and she did not question him. The thought of not being with him troubled her.

Bernardo called one day and asked her to meet him at a waterfront restaurant a few miles from town. She arrived a bit early. Looking at the bay waters, she mulled over why Bernardo had asked to meet her here. Usually, they would meet in his apartment. She looked around. There were few people about. The thought of seeing him always stirred those feelings she had for him. He was fantastic. Many women would have chosen him, but he wanted her.

She saw a car drive in close by and saw him open the door and come towards her. Tall and handsome, he was dressed in dark slacks and a light blue shirt with no tie and sleeves rolled up midway. He did not hurry. He sauntered.

When he finally saw her, he waved and joined her at her table. He greeted her almost like it was a business luncheon. He ordered drinks for them both.

"Sara how are you?" Sara thought how only a few days ago they were having the most wonderful sex and now he was talking like they were two business associates.

"Well," he said "the discussion is about us. Dear Sara, our lives are so different. I don't know if opposites attract or what it is that brings us together. You know how I feel about you. It's not the sex. It's about love. I thought it best today to meet in a public place so we could talk."

Sara started to say something, but he held up his hand and stopped her.

"It is probably important that people come from a similar background and perhaps have similar interests. You have what I call a society life. Essentially, we don't have much in common, but there seems to be a magnet that pulls us together and we can't wait to be together. You go off to your social events and get involved in that which you enjoy. Me—well, I am a soccer guy with very simple tastes."

Then he stopped and looked at her. "I love you. I should not be saying that often, but I've made it pretty clear. You do strange things to me."

She opened her mouth. She had so much she wanted to say. Again he put up his hand and stopped her.

"Don't say anything right now. The fact that you are also married really complicates everything. I find that hard to tolerate, more than anything. You've made it quite clear that you want me as much as I want you. I cannot hug or kiss you publicly. Oh...so many things. We can't go on like this."

As they were talking, another man approached them. Bernardo looked up, "Ted, how are you?"

"Bernardo haven't seen you around much lately. What's cooking? I mean, besides things at your restaurant." He turned to Sara. "And who's the lady?"

"Well, first of all I've been a bit busier than usual at the restaurant. Oh, this is Sara. She will be doing some calligraphy work for me at the restaurant. This is just a business meeting."

Ted turned to Sara, "Watch out for this guy, Sara, he's dangerous." He shook hands with them both and was soon on his way.

"To continue" she said. "You're right. My marriage stands between us."

"If you want me to walk away, say so."

Her one-word reply was measured. "Never."

He controlled himself and simply looked down and twirled the drink he had before him.

"Frankly, if this is not resolved soon, I will have to reluctantly move on" he said solemnly. "I'm thinking of my future and what I want and need. These sometime encounters are fabulous, but that is not what I eventually want for myself. Sara, sweetheart, you have to understand. Do you?"

He stood up for a moment, looked out at the sea. Then once more, he sat down, facing her. "There's a big ocean between us, Sara." Softly, he whispered "I want to marry you and I want us to have a family. I want to be with you forever."

This time she was stunned beyond words. She could not even open her mouth.

Again, he stood up. There was a nervousness to his movements, so rare for him. He had always been in control of situations. On his face there was a sad look. He said, "I have business to take care of today. The solution has to come from you." He looked up to the sky and then down at her. "I repeat, now you know what I want. I'll wait for your answer. But please don't keep me waiting too long."

Sara was crestfallen. Together they left the restaurant. Her feet were like clay and her heart was heavy. Silently, she walked ahead of him to their respective cars.

As they were ready to part, he patted her on her derriere, "Hmm, does that feel good."

Sara turned sharply and angrily said something so unlike her. "Bastard".

He did not look back, but got into his car and drove away.

* * *

Without much more to say, they went their separate ways. He had not seen Sara since their last meeting at the waterfront. It had been several weeks. She had never replied to what he had asked of her. He saw other women, but the encounters were platonic. He tried to make a pleasant evening of the time he spent with them. But he yearned for Sara.

One night he decided to visit the club where she sang. He sat far back so that she would not see him. When she appeared, he was astounded at how pallid she looked. She must be ill, he thought. Sara simply was not herself. He knew her well. Suddenly, he was worried about her.

When the entire program was over, he went to his car, which he had parked adjacent to hers. He waited for her to exit the club. When he saw her walk to her car, she suddenly looked up. He was but a few feet from her. He did not address her by name, but simply said, "What is the matter with you? You look terrible."

Angrily, she replied, "What do you care?"

"Sara, I care." Then he stopped. "Look, get in my car and we can talk."

"What is there to talk about? You said it all when you sent me on my way."

"Sara, I simply asked you to make a decision. However, you never replied. I waited for your answer."

Now Bernardo raised his voice. "Get in my car this minute or I'll start a scene."

"No," she said.

He grabbed her by the arm, opened the passenger side of his car, and pushed her in. "I don't want to hear another word from you until we talk. Understand? We're going to my apartment. I'll take you back to your car when I hear what you have to say."

She was silent as they drove away. She only looked down at her hands.

When they arrived at his apartment, he said "Sit on the other side of that table and tell me what is the matter with you." He looked at her and began again. "Sara, we had a great relationship. You know how I feel about you. Why, I know every inch of that beautiful body of yours." He was going to continue, but she interrupted him.

"Stop it," she screamed. "I'm going to have your baby."

He was astounded at what she had said. "Say that again."

"I'm pregnant with your baby."

His chair fell back as he hurried to her side. He quickly picked her up in his arms. "Sweetheart," he cried. "I am so happy. I don't know how to tell you how I feel right now." He kissed her over and over.

She did not respond nor did she put her arms around him for reassurance.

"Why are you so indifferent?" he queried.

"Easy for you to say. You've gone on your way and now I'm in this condition."

"Sara, I couldn't be happier. I'll never abandon you." Then he hesitated. Anger burned in his eyes. He grasped her by the shoulders. "When were you going to tell me about my baby?" Louder, he continued, "When?"

She looked up at him and began to say, "I..." Then she began to sob. Her sobs continued, as he felt her knees buckle.

He picked her up. Suddenly his tone changed. He was concerned for her health and for the baby.

Then he half smiled and softly said, "When did you go off the pill and when did you conceive?"

"I was no longer on the pill when you returned from your trip."

Sara continued to cry. "What am I going to do? What is going to happen?"

"I said I'll never abandon you."

In his own inimitable way, he hugged her tightly and caressed her reassuringly. She held on to him. "Don't leave me" she cried.

"Oh, my dearest and sweetest Sara, you know you are the love of my life and I'll never want anybody but you." His lips brushed her forehead.

She looked up at him with teary eyes. "Sara, you need to get a divorce. When was the last time you saw your husband?"

"He's been on a two-month mission to the Orient," she replied. "I cannot tell him anything about this."

"Here's what you need to do. Write him, about a divorce. Cite irreconcilable differences. You spend much time apart and have a valid reason. But do not tell him about your condition. He could easily make things difficult for you."

She started to reply. Instead, she yawned. He looked at her face. "Sara, you look tired."

She said, "I tire very easily now."

"Look, get into bed here and rest. You can always leave in the morning."

She did as he suggested and promptly fell asleep.

Before he covered her with a blanket, he gently kissed her on the stomach. She stirred slightly.

When she awakened the next morning, Bernardo told her he would get her breakfast. She was to remain in bed. She did as he said. She sipped her tea and ate the toast which he brought her. Wanly, she smiled at him.

Speaking softly and quite seriously, he sat by her bedside and turned to her. In his lovely accent, Bernardo said, "Possibly, we have nothing in common, my dearest Sara, but you are my heart. Do you understand? You are my heart. I cannot function without you. Maybe I broke the rules in wanting you and loving you, but my heart overruled me. I want you to be my wife. When I go to bed each night, I want you close to me. When I awaken every morning, I want to see you near me."

He stopped for a moment and took her hand in his. "Who knows who determines these matters. From the first moment I saw you I've never wanted anyone but you. I love you fiercely. I want us to be happy. You are going to have our baby. We need to be together. No one will ever love you more than I do. You must understand, Sara."

Then he laid on his back. Gently he picked her up with both hands and placed her body on his chest, so that they were face to face. Looking at her, he said, "I want to feel your heart beating next to mine now. Our baby has to know that there are two loving parents here."

In that moment she saw his fragility and heard the depth of his words. It was so poignant and touched her in a way she had never felt before. Suddenly, she knew what she had known for so long. She wanted to cry. Instead she said quietly as she choked back the tears, "Bernardo, you've loved me from the beginning. You continued to love me even when I was confused and skittish, and when I could not make a decision. I did not want to give up my life style, even though I was unhappy." Now the tears welled in her eyes. "Darling, thank you for finding me. Oh, I love you so much." As she hugged him tightly, he silently buried his face in her neck

There was no doubt in Sara's mind now that she only wanted him. She was madly in love with him. As he had often said, she was his.

* * *

For her last show at the club, Sara asked Bernardo to attend. He hesitated. Sara was insistent, "Please, darling, it's my last show and I want you there."

He smiled at her. "Okay. I'll be there, but just for you."

None of the trio nor the club's employees knew Bernardo. Sara, however, wanted him to have a front row seat. No one questioned why.

When it was time for her to sing, she came out in a black gown cut low in front. Her eyes were sparkling. She wore his pearl pendant. Sara had chosen a series of love songs which she sang in that lush voice of hers. Not once did she look at him. Then he heard her pronounce to the audience, "Lastly, here is a beautiful song." She turned to the trio and nodded. They knew what she would now sing. This time she faced Bernardo. His look was one of anticipation. She began to sing, "Unforgettable, that's what you are...." As she continued from there, he looked at her in the loving way he often did and their hearts locked. The song was just for him.

Bernardo looked at how beautiful she was. He fingered his drink and recalled this was where he had first seen her. This was also the place where he decided he wanted to know her better and had to have her. It had been a roller coaster ride for them, but he was full of hope that now they both were in a good place. With her pregnancy, she had truly blossomed. He was so proud of her and happy with the news of a baby in their future.

When she finished her set, she told the people who had listened to her sing that it was her last show for a while. As they applauded, she bowed. Instead of exiting back stage, she stepped down to where he sat. He was surprised. As she sat next to him, he took her hand and kissed it. "I love you so so much" he whispered. The applause continued with some additional cheering,

Where it had all started, it was now ending. A new phase in their lives was coming.

* * *

EPILOGUE

Sara got her divorce with little acrimony. As soon as possible, she and Bernardo found a justice of the peace and were quietly married. At that moment, he took her face in his hands, "Sara, now you are completely mine." They were deliriously happy. "I'm sorry we can't toast this occasion with champagne because of your condition, but I'll make it up to you" he promised.

"When the baby is born" she replied. He nodded in agreement.

After their marriage they returned to his apartment to live. It would have to accommodate them until they could think of what they were going to do next. With the baby set to arrive soon, they needed larger quarters. For now, this was it. Everything had happened so rapidly. However, Bernardo was thinking ahead. He had a family now and they required certain needs.

"Sara" he said one day shortly thereafter "could you do some calligraphy work for me?" Sara, of course, said yes. She needed to keep busy while awaiting their baby. Bernardo not only was so happy, but so caring of her.

Again, he talked to her about what he needed for his restaurant. Sara was good at what she did. She knew instantly what he wanted. One early afternoon she sat in a booth and proceeded with her work. Bernardo was busy with the few people who came in later. Among them were the ladies from the nearby hospital who frequented his restaurant often.

After he greeted them in his usual affable way, they perused the menu. As they came in often, they pretty much knew what they wanted. There were five of them. One looked up and saw Sara across the room, with her head down working.

As Bernardo waited for their order, she said, "Bernardo, who is that lovely young lady?"

Bernardo quickly answered, "That's Sara, my calligrapher. She's doing some work for me. Want to meet her?" Yes, they said. He called Sara over.

"Sara, I'd like you to meet the nice ladies from the hospital who are my best customers."

Sara smiled and shook each of their hands, "Bernardo always says great things about all of you."

Then they looked askance as Bernardo put one arm around Sara's shoulder and the other on her stomach, "Sara is also my wife and we're awaiting our first baby."

Then came a babble of voices. "When did this happen?" "You never told us you were married." "How long has this been going on?" One jokingly said, "We were taking bets on which of us you would take out." Suddenly the tenor changed. "What great news."

Bernardo laughed at the cackling. "You all didn't think I spent all my time in this restaurant. There was a life for me out there. And this beautiful woman is the one I chose." He hugged Sara again. Then he stopped and continued, "Okay, for being so nice to my wife, today you get free dessert."

This was when everyone laughed and relaxed. Sara was amused at how they were carrying on. She turned on her heel and walked back to her work booth.

* * *

He held her hand and comforted her throughout her labor. When Sara finally delivered their baby, Bernardo cried unabashedly. He kissed Sara and said, "Thank you for our baby and making my life complete. I love you so much." Holding his daughter, he looked with wonder at their beautiful little girl. They named her Bettina, after Bernardo's mother.

For weeks after, Bernardo watched Sara as she mothered their baby. He was bursting with pride. They had created something that was part of them both. As Sara nursed the baby, she turned to her husband, "Darling, isn't she beautiful?" With adoring eyes, he replied, "You are both beautiful." Then he would take his daughter in his arms. He burped her and cuddled her. Then Sara would hear him whisper over and over, "My beautiful baby. My beautiful baby." Sara smiled at his behavior as a new father.

Eventually, they talked about moving to Europe to live. A new beginning, Bernardo thought. Sara was amenable to the idea. Her language skills were good. Besides, she would go wherever he chose.

Without concern about the right time to leave, they simply moved to Europe. Bernardo sold his restaurant and soon they were on their way. In the northwest part of Italy was a charming little resort town. With his cooking skills they sought a restaurant or small hotel that would fit their needs. On a little street they found what they wanted. A small hotel with sixteen rooms by the water's edge. Sara could handle hotel reservations and sundry other things. Bernardo was at home in the kitchen. It took a bit of work to ready everything for the upcoming season. There were people to hire, along with a nanny for their baby. The enthusiasm was there for both of them.

They also needed to do some advertising and get in touch with travel agents all over Europe (in the United Kingdom, Germany, the Scandinavian countries, etc.). They had some success. Perhaps, in the future, word of mouth would provide them with a clientele and loyal following. They hoped that matters would soon begin to fall into place. It was a question of time.

The first season at their small hotel provided some challenges, as they were new to the scene. Sara was quite good at gauging people's needs despite language differences. Their clientele came from various parts of Europe.

Bernardo had hired a young man as his sous chef who was not only familiar with the area, but had some innovative ideas for the meals they served daily. People's needs and tastes varied, but they were there to serve them well.

They hired a nanny from Ireland named Teresa for their baby. This enabled Bernardo and Sara to tend to their new business. Sometimes Teresa would take over the front desk from Sara. She was a pleasant girl and enjoyed meeting new people. Since Bernardo's and Sara's apartment was only three flights up, it was easy for them to return there at day's end.

Overall, the people that stayed at their hotel had few complaints and this pleased everyone.

After the season was over, Bernardo and Sara were able to resume a more leisurely pace and go over ideas to better their nascent business. All the hard work seemed to be paying off. They were tired, but elated at this new juncture in their lives. In recalling all the people who had come and gone during their first season as hoteliers, one stood out for Bernardo. The Swedish lady.

As Bernardo walked through the foyer of his small hotel, a beautiful statuesque blond approached him. She was wearing a tight white dress, he noticed. In fact, she was stunning and he looked her over more than once. She looked Scandinavian to him, probably Swedish. As she confronted him, she asked, "Excuse me, I'm new here. What is there to do at night?"

"Well, there are bars along the way, as well as a night club" he replied.

He realized she was coming on to him, so he played along.

"Is there something in particular you like to do?" he asked sweetly.

"I like to dance a lot. Some place nice and cozy, perhaps."

"Hmm" he whispered to her "We certainly could arrange something to please you."

She whispered back, "Sounds delicious to me."

"I tell you what, let's ask the receptionist what we can do for you."

He smiled at her. She was definitely interested in this handsome man. He could probably be great fun for her tonight and show her a good time.

As they approached the receptionist, he said, "Could you help this lovely lady make some plans for a great night on the town? Oh, by the way what is your name?"

"Lila" she breathlessly replied.

"What a lovely name" he said. "Lila, this is my wife, Sara. She'll be more than happy to help you."

Bernardo turned on his heel and walked away. Sara knew what to do.

* * *

One day an English gentleman came to the front desk and addressed Sara,

"My name is Hawthorne. I have a reservation for myself and my wife."

Sara checked the listings. "Yes, of course, Mr. Hawthorne, we have you down for one week for you and your wife. Here we go, Room 15 on the third floor. The elevator is there to your right." She handed him the room keys.

Mr. Hawthorne smiled at Sara and said, "You must be American?"

"Yes," replied Sara.

As Bernardo was returning to his kitchen, he walked by them.

"Mr. Hawthorne, this is my husband," she said.

Bernardo smiled. "My pleasure, Mr. Hawthorne."

Mr. Hawthorne noticed Bernardo's accent. "How did an Italian man marry an American girl?"

Bernardo replied, "We met in the States some years ago." Then Bernardo continued, "Actually, we had nothing in common."

As Bernardo walked away, he turned to Sara and winked at her. There was a time when he thought she would not be completely his. He was a very happy man. She was the love of his life.

Sara smiled back at her husband. Now she had everything.

Promises Made

PROMISES MADE

eth ran up the stairs, heading for her bedroom. In her haste, she stumbled a couple of times. When she opened the door to her room, she hurried to her bed, threw herself on it, and began sobbing. How could this be happening to me, she thought? Perfection did not exist, but still for some years it had been perfect.

Beth had been married almost eleven years to Drew. He was an architect and successful in his field. They lived a good life. He had even designed their home. Their friends all thought it was so elegant. Entertaining in their home was something their friends invariably enjoyed and looked forward to. They traveled together, when they could. Although they had no children, overall, it was an idyllic life.

As to work, Beth was an appointment secretary in a large medical office. It was a part-time job, enabling her to take time off to travel with Drew.

When her sobbing eased, she sat up and went over what had occurred this day. She had run into her old friend, Lucy, who insisted they have coffee then and there. They found a coffee shop nearby which allowed them to slowly savor their beverage. Lucy, who was a stay-at-home mom to three children, knew everything about everyone. Their friend, Olivia, had become pregnant, but had miscarried. Lucy insisted they should visit with her sometime. Jeff and Helen had just returned from a month's cruise in the Pacific. On and on she went. Although Beth was not the gossipy type, she, of course, enjoyed all the news Lucy provided.

"So, how are things with you and Drew?" Lucy asked.

"Very well" said Beth. "We're thinking of adding a pool to our property. Should be fun, since we both love to swim."

"Hope you have some pool parties" interjected Lucy.

"But, of course, Lucy."

"By the way, doesn't Drew have a young colleague in his office named Dana?"

"Yes" said Beth.

"I've often seen them at lunch at the Hotel Biltmore?" Lucy continued.

So like Lucy to make much ado about nothing. "Oh, Lucy, you know in business that often happens. People continue their discussions at lunch. Drew loves me and that's that" she said smugly.

"Yes, but do they also get in the elevator together and ride to the tenth floor, where all the rooms are?"

Beth's heart skipped a beat. She had to be nonchalant if not for her own sake, but because of Lucy's insinuation. She took a breath and concluded her conversation with Lucy by saying, "Don't make a romance out of business. Many men go out with their female business partners." She hesitated and stared her down. "Now tell me about what's going on in your life."

Lucy sighed and prattled on about the adorable things her children did. Beth really did not hear one word she said. She only smiled now and then.

Drew never gave any indication that he did not love her. Coming home each night he would give her a brief synopsis of his work that day. Both of them naturally thought their sex life was very good. Should she take credence in Lucy's ramblings? Could she conjure up some unknown bad aspects of their marital life? Sometime people could be so cruel about what they imagine is happening. But then Lucy had nothing better to do.

Suddenly, Beth realized it was all nonsense. Lucy thrived on gossip. Beth pulled herself together, arose from bed, washed her face, and went to prepare dinner. When Drew returned home, he approached her and kissed her sweetly.

Suddenly, all those dire thoughts had left her mind.

One day Beth called Drew at work, something she rarely did. It was about 3 p.m. She was told he was out. She stared into space.

That night when Drew returned home, she mentioned her call. Drew simply said he had been out on a job.

There were moments when she scoffed at the idea of her husband being unfaithful. However, Lucy had put a bee in her bonnet. She tried to put the thought out of her mind. She knew Drew so well. There had never been any disharmony in their marriage.

Several weeks later her friend Allison suggested lunch. She said that the lobster Newburg at the Hotel Biltmore was quite good. Then she added, "Shall we lunch there tomorrow?" "Fine by me" said Beth.

Lunch with Allison was always fun. She was a travel agent who would regale her with the clients she dealt with and the trips she took.

When Allison excused herself and went to the ladies room after lunch, Beth sat in a secluded part of the foyer behind some fronds on display. Gazing about she was flabbergasted to see her husband and a young lady (it looked like Dana) approach the elevator. She was about to rise and greet them, but she noticed they looked at each other in a very chummy way. She stopped and watched them get in the elevator. They were smiling sweetly at each other. The elevator rose to the tenth floor and stopped. She was aghast.

When Allison rejoined her, Beth's face was ashen. "What's the matter, Beth? You don't look well."

Beth gasped and said, "Must have been the lobster Newburg. I need to get home." Without further explanation, she ran out the door to her car.

Once home, she roamed around her home aimlessly. She did not know what to think. Lucy had been right. Beth took an anti-anxiety pill, lay down on her bed, and eventually fell asleep.

When she awakened, she heard Drew calling out to her. The sun was beginning to set. When she sat up, she realized it was late in the day. She did not know how to handle this situation. She needed to formulate a plan to address this matter with Drew. Things had to be put in perspective.

Drew scooted up the stairs to their bedroom. "Honey" he called out. He noticed her pained look. "Are you okay?"

"I went to lunch with Allison and had lobster newburg. It made me sick." She looked pallid.

"Can I do anything? An antacid or something like that?"

"No" she said quietly, without looking at him. "I'm going to stay in bed a bit. Take care of yourself for dinner."

"Very well" he shouted after her, as he returned downstairs.

Later when Beth collected her thoughts, she slowly walked down to their kitchen. Drew was eating soup.

When he looked up at her, he said, "Better?"

All of Beth's plans about what she would say to Drew about this horrifying situation went out the window. She blurted out, "I want a divorce."

Drew gulped on his soup. "What are you saying? A divorce?"

"I want a divorce" she repeated louder.

"Are you joking? Stop this nonsense. I've been waiting all day to get my hands on your sweet flesh."

Angrily, she replied, "I bet."

"Oh, oh, bad day for my beautiful wife." He walked over to where she was standing and attempted to take her in his arms.

"Stop that" she said loudly.

"Teasing me, are you?"

"Not at all. No teasing tonight."

"Are we having an argument?" he asked. Then he stepped back and looked at her again. "What has happened?"

"No" she emphasized. "I am furious and embarrassed."

Then Drew got serious. "Whatever is the matter, honey?"

"How many floors does the Hotel Biltmore have?"

"What does that have to do with your attitude tonight?"

Beth continued, "Everything must look lovely from the tenth floor." She was seething.

Drew's face turned ashen. "It is a hotel, you know." He was becoming defensive. Then he again turned and began to walk away from her.

Now her voice got louder and angrier. "Don't walk away from me, you fraud."

Drew knew he had to confront her and he had to do it now. Slowly, he turned around and walked back to her. Before he could say a word, she began sobbing again and saying, "I want a divorce."

She was alluding to something. Suddenly Drew knew what she was talking about. She had seen him with Dana. He tried standing his ground. Then he stared at her, saying nothing. Quietly, he said, "I don't know what you are foolishly saying." He was trying any ploy.

"Foolish, you say." Louder still, "Foolish!"

He turned back to her. "Okay, lay it on me."

"That's the word 'lay'. Were you laying her this afternoon?" She rushed on with her words. "I saw you and her come off the elevator in the hotel with a smug look on your faces."

Drew began, "I..."

Beth quickly interrupted. "Is that what you do afternoons? Screw her for lunch?"

"Who...who are you talking about?"

"That sexy Dana from your office." Beth was getting angrier. "Stop playing games with me."

Beth thought her head would explode. She ran back up the stairs to their bedroom.

Drew's first instinct was to run after her. However, after he had taken a few steps, he stopped. What was he going to say? Beth had obviously seen them coming off the elevator at the hotel with that satisfied look on their faces.

He sat down in the nearest chair and placed his head in his hands. God, what had he done to Beth. Never did he think he would be discovered. What to do? What to do? He couldn't deny it. Beth had been pretty explicit in having seen them. What a dilemma. He had never done this before. After all their years together, he had never hurt her like this

Drew walked back up to their bedroom. Not only did he want to explain, but he had to reassure her. "Beth, don't say that. You know that I love you so much. I fell under her spell. Please forgive me. Please! Don't mention divorce. There were promises made on our wedding day and I won't allow you to break them. I made a big mistake. I'm not infallible. Promises made. Remember?"

Beth continued crying.

"Those promises we made were that we would always stay together. Forever." After eleven years he suddenly did not know how to right this tragedy. Out of the blue, he said, "How about counseling? Maybe we can go back to the wonderful relationship we have always had and maybe make it even better." The thought had suddenly come to him. Marriage counseling. A third party might enable them to right this matter. Oh, how his conscience bothered him.

He sat on the edge of the bed and tried to cuddle her. When he touched her, he realized how much he loved her. He couldn't lose her. He said it aloud to her, "I can't lose you." Then he became pragmatic. "Look on the computer for a marriage counselor we can both consult. Okay?" Beth nodded, although she continued to whimper.

When he arose, he was bedraggled. He covered her and went downstairs. A stiff drink was what he needed. As he hurriedly downed his drink, he knew there had to be a resolution to this situation. He needed to save his marriage. God, how he needed a good night's sleep after this harrowing day.

The next morning Beth arose from bed, still fully clothed. Drew was next to her, also fully clothed. Neither had changed into bed clothes, but had fallen asleep completely exhausted by the events of the previous day and night.

Beth went to her computer scrolling and looking under the heading "Marriage Counselors". They needed someone to help them out of this morass. Each of them had a heart that ached at what had transpired.

* * *

There were three of them in the room. Beth sat to one side in a leather chair looking up to the ceiling. Drew sat on a leather couch nervously staring at the woman in front of him behind a large desk. Her name was Mrs. Long. She was about 60 years old. She was the marriage counselor. Looking at both of them, she said, "You must both speak freely here if you want to salvage your marriage."

Drew murmured, "I do. I do."

Beth continued looking up at the ceiling and sighing now and then, but saying nothing.

Drew spoke first. "Mrs. Long, I want you to know that I love Beth very much. I feel with each year of our marriage I've come to love her more and more. She is the last person I would hurt. I made a mistake—a big one."

Beth simply moved around in her chair, again not saying a word.

"Do you want to continue, Drew?" said Mrs. Long.

"The young lady in my office is named Dana. An attractive young woman. Frankly, someone most men would look at twice. A couple of the young architects in my office approached her for a date, but she seemingly rebuffed them. Even some of the men I did business with were also interested, but they got nowhere with her. To me she was simply another of my workers. Now and again I would notice her coming on to me, but I figured she was trying to make points insofar as her work went. Of course, she knew I was married, but this did not dissuade her from whatever her goals were.

"Like many of the other workers in my office, I would continue my business discussions with them at lunch sometime. I did the same with her. Remember, taking her to lunch was only a continuation of what was going on in the workplace. Even her subtle overtures were flattering. Suddenly, I was looking forward to our luncheons. In that atmosphere, I seemed to be more at ease.

"Being a normal man, I began to envision kissing her and touching her intimately. Before I go further, may I say Beth still turns me on. She is a beautiful woman. Look at her." He turned to face her.

Before he could go further, Beth sobbed quietly. Drew got up to go to her, but she would not let him touch her. "Honey" he said, "don't torment yourself."

Mrs. Long interrupted. "Beth, do you want to say something?"

Looking directly at her, Beth quietly said, "I've always loved Drew. We were soulmates. We had a happy marriage. Despite not having children, all was right in our lives. I can't believe all that has happened here."

Drew looked down. He wanted to reassure her, but felt it would evoke more tears. Still he had to say something to repair his relationship with her, "Beth, honey, it will never happen again. Please, please, forgive me. Let's go someplace for a second honeymoon. Anywhere you want."

After further discussion of the current situation, Mrs. Long coughed to get their attention. She looked at her office clock. The session was concluding now; it had been almost an hour. "This week I want you both to find the good things in your lives and dwell on that. Try to work at being amicable with each other. Next week I hope you can be here at the same time. Is that okay with each of you?"

They both nodded and rose to leave. Each had come in his own car.

Once home, they said little. Married so long, but now there was an awkwardness there. Each was afraid of saying the wrong thing.

Drew went to his computer to check his messages. Very sweetly, he turned to her and said, "Do you want to prepare dinner while I go jogging around the block a few times?"

"Fine" she said.

Beth went to the kitchen to ready something for dinner. She needed a sense of normalcy now, especially here in the confines of her own home.

After he returned and showered, he walked into the kitchen and said, "Smells good. Is it spaghetti and your great homemade sauce?" He attempted to smile at her.

"Yes" she said. He had chosen a red wine from their wine rack to complete the dinner. However, sitting across from one another, they were silent as they ate their meal. After he had placed the dishes and stemware in the dishwasher, he said, "Beth, I have more work to complete on my computer. Do you mind?"

Again the response was only one word, "No."

Since she had discovered his infidelity, she had been sleeping in the guest room. Drew was hurt, but he realized she would not want to be intimate while she was still inconsolable.

Turning on his computer he began thinking how in the past their return from work most days had been so pleasant. Often, they would get out of their clothes, get into their hot tub, and with a glass of wine in hand, they would talk at length of the day's events, laugh about some inane matters, or make plans for upcoming events. This was a rather unique way of relaxing. After they emerged from the tub, they would dry off, retire to their bedroom, and make love. Beth never failed to turn him on. Then it was dinner. They may have done things backwards, but there was no one to account to.

For some time they talked about installing a pool on their property because they were fond of the water. Loving the water as they did, they also kept a small boat at the local yacht club for excursions in the immediate area.

But now Drew turned to the work at hand. He had to keep going.

* * *

The following week they returned to Mrs. Long's office to continue their discussion, with hopes of a good resolution.

"How did it all start, Drew?" said Mrs. Long.

"I repeat, the luncheons were relaxing. I enjoyed Dana's company. We often began to discuss other things instead of our work projects. We laughed and reminisced. Our luncheons became longer. Since it was my company, there were no questions about my longer absences from the office.

"One afternoon, while we were enjoying our meal, from across the table I felt her bare leg move far up my trouser. Although I was startled, I was also aroused. Maybe, it was the wine, or something. I don't know. Silently, we looked at each other and she smiled. I got up. 'I'm getting a room right now' I said. She looked at me in that coquette fashion. She did not object. When I returned to our table a few minutes later, all I said was 'Room 1004'. I paid the luncheon tab and arose on my way to the elevator and the tenth floor.

"When shortly thereafter she arrived, we were in each other's arms and disrobed quickly. Yes, she told me she had been waiting a long time for this. She proved quite sexy and I enjoyed it all. It was a new experience.

"When our afternoon tryst was over, we moved together to the elevator and to the ground floor. It was the pleasure of the moment."

Then Drew stopped and pleadingly looked at Beth. "Honey, it is so embarrassing to say all this in your presence. God, how could I have been so foolish. Beth, please say you'll forgive me. Trust me, it won't happen again. I love you so much and I don't want to jeopardize that which is so precious to me. In fact, precious to us."

Beth moved uneasily in her chair and looked so forlorn.

"Aren't you going to say something, Beth?" asked Mrs. Long.

Slowly, Beth answered, "You think these things happen to other people only, but they don't. We're all vulnerable. I am so hurt and mortified. How long will it take me to forgive him? It will always haunt me and be there in my mind."

Mrs. Long interrupted her. "If your marriage was so great and you want everything to be as before, well I doubt it will happen. But consideration of each other will make all that happened seem unreal after a time. You cannot take each other for granted and you have to know that in this imperfect world there are many temptations. If you want Drew back, Beth, you have to make the effort."

"I know" she said. "I know."

Then Mrs. Long turned her attention to Drew. "How often did you meet with Dana?"

Drew hesitated. He coughed. He knew he had to clear the slate. "We met three times."

Beth gasped and placed her head in her hands.

Drew looked at her longingly. He sighed and continued, "I don't know what Dana thought would come of it, but I began to feel guilty. God, my wife is so sexy and fabulous in bed." He continued with his narration, with questions interspersed by Mrs. Long now and again.

The session continued. The questions and answers by Drew were awkward. They were there for the prescribed time. Then when their time was up, Beth and Drew arose and left the office without saying anything to each other. Each drove away in his own automobile, although they were both returning to the same place. To their home.

For several weeks they attended the sessions with Mrs. Long. One day soon thereafter Drew looked at Beth and said, "Can't we resolve this on our own now?"

Beth was slow to respond. Finally, she looked at him and said, "I think we can do it. I don't want to lose all the special things that there have been in our lives for eleven years."

Drew was elated at what she said. "Trust me, honey, I'll never hurt you again." He stood up, went to where she was sitting, and pulled her up to him. He hugged her and kissed her tenderly.

He then turned to Mrs. Long, "Thanks for your help. I think—in fact, I know—everything will be all right now. Please send me your bill."

After that last session, they walked out the door together. Drew took Beth's hand in his and squeezed it. This time she did not pull away.

As they walked to their automobile, Drew turned to her. Before she could say anything, he said, "I have something important to tell you in order to rectify this problem. I'm going to ask Dana to leave the company."

Beth looked up at him, anticipating what else he would say.

"I'll tell her we are downsizing and ask her to look elsewhere for work. I'll give her a bonus."

Before Beth could reply, Drew put up his hand. "I don't know if she'll be happy or not, but she needs to go away so I can continue my work without distraction. What do you think?"

Quietly Beth said, "You won't see her if she moves elsewhere?"

"Absolutely not. I repeat, there were promises made to you long ago and I intend to keep them."

* * *

Beth and Drew were in their kitchen preparing dinner. Since Beth was a good baker, she had already prepared a beautiful jelly roll cake with a great chocolate ganache filling. Of the two of them, Drew was the better cook. He was making baked short ribs with cognac, along with roasted vegetables.

As they worked together, each at his own specialty, the phone in the other room rang.

"Honey," said Drew, "will you answer that? I'm about ready to remove everything from the oven."

"Okay" said Beth. She hurried to the phone in the adjacent room.

"Hello" she said.

A familiar male voice on the other end said, "Sweetheart, I haven't heard from you in some time."

Beth was startled. Her heart skipped a beat. His voice on the other end of the phone made her pause. Because she was not answering him, he said, "Am I to deduce that you cannot talk right now?"

"Yes" she replied.

"Listen, tomorrow at the hotel at 1 p.m. I want to see you. I need to see you. Okay?" Then he hung up.

When she returned to the kitchen, Drew turned to her, "Who was that?" She was slow to answer. He repeated, "Who was that?"

"Telemarketer" said Beth.

He turned back to what he was doing. "How annoying."

"Yes" she gulped.

Barely thinking of the dessert she had prepared, she automatically pulled out a pretty platter from her cupboard and placed her dessert thereon.

Drew turned to her smiling and said, "Cake looks wonderful. You've always been a great baker. In fact, you've always been so good at whatever you do." He was flattering her.

She was hardly listening to him. All she could think of was the call she had just received. Tomorrow she would be in the arms of her lover.

* * *

That night as she readied for bed, Drew approached Beth as she headed again for the guest room. Softly, he said, "Beth, honey, please sleep with me tonight. I miss that so much." He caressed her cheek and then her arms. "Please" he repeated.

Beth could not help but say what she was feeling. "I've missed being in our bed with you."

He took her by the hand and up the stairs. Without saying much, they were soon together where they had always been for eleven years. He was very gentle and loving with her even though his passion was great. She was surprised at how he was treating her in those moments. It was all so very special and strangely enough, beautiful. She felt his love as never before. She turned to him and said softly, "I had forgotten how wonderful this could be between us."

"Honey, what can I say?" he finally said. "With you I always get the utmost pleasure." Then he faced her and said, "Let's spend all day tomorrow somewhere by ourselves. What do you think?" He still held her tightly.

She pulled herself out of his arms. Beth looked at her husband. Hesitantly, she said, "I have a one o'clock appointment tomorrow." Then she turned away from him.

Beth began ruminating. She had gotten back at her husband by doing what he had done to her. She had done the unthinkable. While going to the marriage counselor no less, she had gotten involved with another man. She had called Drew a fraud. She was more than that. Having an affair after Drew had admitted to his transgressions was unconscionable of her. Absolutely, unconscionable!

Was it an act of recrimination on her part? Anger, perhaps? It was all beginning to haunt her. She had to quickly rectify it all before she lost him forever.

How could she? How? She loved Drew dearly. She did not want to lose him. She looked at him now and moved closer to him. Her arms went around his waist and she placed her head on his chest. This all had to end. They had to go back to their beginning. Drew

71

was right. Life would not always be perfect for them, but surely trust could return again to their lives. There had been promises made long ago.

One moment later she turned her face up to him. Gulping on her words, she said, "I'm going to break my appointment tomorrow. Let's go off on our boat for two or three days. Away from everyone." She looked at him imploringly.

Drew hugged her tightly, kissing the top of her head. He could not have been more pleased at her suggestion.

Ageless Love

AGELESS LOVE

ena's Diner was an ideal spot for coffee drinkers. It was right off the highway. And people took advantage of that. With their hurried lives and all, people stopped there for a morning cup of coffee. Many would be going to their jobs or to school or wherever. Everything was rush, rush, rush. There was a large variety of beverages, including espresso (a good pick-me-up). The several tables that seated four were quickly filled up for those that could linger. Others would buy their beverage and would soon be out the door. Those that lingered had to be lucky to find a seat. Naturally, one ended up sitting with strangers. Often these people would simply greet each other and might say a few words, while there were those who did not. It was just a spot to have their coffee leisurely. Some read the morning paper or updated themselves on their technological devices. It was just read, drink, and run.

Gayle was one of those who came in most mornings and did not hurry. She was retired and had the entire day to herself to do as she wished. At home, however, she spent part of the day painting at her easel in her studio. It was that which gave her great satisfaction. It had also been her life's work and she was good at it. It enabled her to make a living during her working life.

Before sitting down to have her coffee at the diner, she would look around at the other people. Invariably, she observed those who drank, rushed out the door, to be replaced by others. It was a varied group performing an American ritual. Although this particular day was a bit dreary, nothing changed. She sipped her coffee and continued reading from the little booklet of poems she had brought with her.

"Excuse me, madam, is this seat taken?"

When Gayle looked up, she saw a slender man addressing her. She guessed he was about 55 years of age. More or less.

"No, no. They are all available. Please sit down."

"Thanks" he said, as he laid his coffee on the table and sat down. "Miserable day, no?"

"Well, when you live in New England long enough you never know about the weather. Sometimes you even get snow in March. Are you from this area?"

"Yes, I am and you're right about the weather." People always did that. As an opener, they talked about the weather. He brought the cup up to his lips and gazed at her. "Aren't you hurrying off to work?" he asked.

"Oh, no, I'm retired. I was self-employed for many years. The clock was never my master."

He laughed. "Good for you". He took another sip, but still gazing at her intently. "May I ask what you do...or did?"

"I've been an artist for many years and still have my own studio."

"Sounds wonderful. What do you paint?"

"Usually, landscapes, but I paint a variety of things. Frankly, it depends on my mood."

"Sorry to ask, but were you able to make a decent living with your work?"

"Yes, I've managed, thank you."

"Excuse me, my name is Justin. And yours?"

"Gayle" she replied.

"Nice to meet you, Gayle. He hesitated. "I noticed the small cup of coffee. Are you having espresso?"

"Yes, I often order it. It certainly wakes me up."

"I guess so. For me, it's just regular with cream and sugar."

"Aren't you hurrying off to work like the others hereabouts?"

"No, I'm an English teacher. I have time."

Gayle was polite "How nice. Young people these days are so busy with all those new devices whereby they abbreviate what they have to say, and then rush along with that mode of communication and virtually no face-to-face conversation. How sad."

"Often, it's a chore for me to get my students off those devices and give me a complete and grammatically correct sentence."

She laughed quietly. How true that was. She tried returning to her booklet of poems, but Justin continued talking. When she realized it was fruitless to read, she closed her book.

"Do you live nearby?" he asked.

"Yes, I do. A little morning walk and I'm quickly here."

"Exercise is always good for all of us, Me, I just rush off to the gym."

Looking around he noticed people were still coming and going from the coffee shop, but it was beginning to peter out. Dena's Diner did a good morning business. He stopped talking and turned to his newspaper. "I guess I had better get up to date as to what's going on in this world of ours." He folded the paper and began to read the front page; then he went on to the second page; and so on.

Gayle drank her coffee. She looked him over. Nicely dressed; attractive; and well spoken. What she did not notice was that as he went from page to page, he too was observing her. She had such a lovely demeanor about her, he thought, was nicely dressed, and an attractive woman. He couldn't guess her age, but believed she was somewhere in her sixties. Nice lady to talk to. Interesting to get to know better.

When she arose to leave, he said, "Have a good day. Hope to see you again. I'm here most mornings. You?"

"I try to get here most days, unless I have something more pressing to take care of" she said, as she turned away from the table.

Justin couldn't help but notice that she was simply but elegantly dressed. She had an air about her that intrigued him. He hadn't met too many women here or elsewhere that had evoked his interest. In fact, since his divorce, he had hardly dated at all. He'd try to get here earlier tomorrow so as to have a longer conversation with her. Then he turned back to his newspaper, as he slowly drank his coffee.

True to his word, he did get there earlier the following day. Gayle was not there. He was somewhat disappointed. However, he ordered his coffee, sat down, and began to read while sipping his beverage. He had taken the one remaining seat that there was in the diner. He smiled at the people sitting at his table. Each was engrossed in a newspaper or one of the technological devices that had become so commonplace. Lots of people here today, he thought. Obviously, this was the early morning crowd.

When he slowly finished his coffee, he rolled up his newspaper, stood up, and prepared to leave the diner. Then she walked in. As she headed for the line at the counter to order her drink, he walked up to her with a smile on his face, "Good morning, Gayle." She looked up. "Justin, a very good morning to you too." "Your timing couldn't be better," he said. "I was going to have myself another cup of coffee." Just a little white lie, he thought. "Shall I get us a table?" She saw there were a couple of empty tables. "That would be nice."

Justin was happy he had caught her in time this day. As they sat down and began drinking their coffee, Gayle turned to him, "Aren't you married, Justin?"

"No" he replied. "I'm divorced. I was married for three years, but it simply did not work out. What about you?"

"Well, I've been widowed for over four years. My husband was killed by a drunken driver as he was returning home from a business trip. Terrible news to get when the police come to your door."

"Sorry" he said. For several minutes there was silence. Justin smiled at her in a half-hearted way. "It's hard to pick up a conversation when the news you've just received is not pleasant." He quickly changed the subject. She had finished her coffee. He said, "Can I get you another cup of coffee, Gayle?"

"No, I'm okay for now."

When he returned to their table, he began by saying, "This time I changed my order. I got myself a latte. Have you ever tried one?"

"Justin, let's not make things awkward. What is past, is past."

"I agree" he said. This time he squeezed her hand. "You have nice soft hands."

"Are you going to flatter me now?"

"Okay, okay. Let's go back to square one."

"What are your plans for today?"

"After class, I'm going to a short conference in town."

"That will keep you busy." She rose from her seat. "There is some painting I want to do."

"Gayle, can I walk you home? I have time."

"If you like. My morning began busily and now I have more to do."

It was a sunny morning and they walked silently. He knew her home was nearby. When he left her at her door, he said, "Have a good day." Gayle smiled at him. He turned and walked away. There was more he wanted to say, but today it had been necessarily brief.

So it happened that most mornings Gayle and Justin would run into each other at the coffee shop. Some mornings they were able to share the same table; other times with the plethora of people, they would be seated at different tables. Invariably, she would be there first. When they sat apart, there would simply be a morning greeting. If they were lucky to be seated at the same table, they would talk about a variety of things. Actually, Justin enjoyed their conversations, which he often attacked with enthusiasm. Gayle was always subdued. Because they could discuss a variety of subjects, he was energized with and by her. Although he also thought she was what he told himself "an exciting woman".

One particular morning as they sat together, each reading a different article, Justin turned to her and said, "Gayle, could I take you out to dinner Saturday night?" For Gayle the invitation came out of the blue. Before she could reply, he continued, "I'd like to spend more time with you and this coffee time is much too brief. You can always see people standing, waiting to take our seats."

Gayle looked around. It was true that some mornings Dena's Diner was filled to capacity, with people looking for an empty seat.

Gayle turned back to Justin, "You're right about the crowd." Then she hesitated. "But, why would you want to take me out?"

"If I said simply that I want to, would that suffice?"

"Justin, you're sweet, but..."

He interrupted her, "Gayle, it's just a guy asking for a date with a lovely woman. It's either yes or no."

Gayle really did not know how to respond. Yes, she always enjoyed being with him. As to saying no, she truly did not want to refuse him. She enjoyed his company. "What do you have in mind?"

"Dinner at a Chinese or Italian restaurant or wherever you like to eat."

Dates at her age were extremely rare. Bravely she said, "Yes, I would like that."

Gayle could see how happy he was at her answer. Justin was elated. "Very well, Saturday at 6:30 p.m. I'll pick you up. Got to dash today, so I cannot linger. Now, don't accept any invitations from the next guy that sits here." He took her hand as he walked away. Gayle's smile was a broad one.

At 6:30 p.m. on Saturday evening, he was at her front door. When she opened it, his eyes focused on her and then traveled from her head to her toes. She was dressed in black slacks, a bright blue blouse, and carrying a colorful shawl in her hands. "Good evening, Justin. Welcome. Please come in." He stepped in the foyer, took the small bouquet of flowers he had brought with him, handed them to her and only said one word. "Stunning!"

When she took the flowers from him, she smelled them and said, "What a lovely fragrance. Thank you." She hurried around, looking for a vase, filled it with water, and placed everything on a side table. She then placed the shawl around her shoulders, and said, "For the flowers and the compliment, many thanks. Are we ready to go?" He took her hand, smiled at her, and said, "Yes."

Once ensconced in his car, he turned to her and said again, "You look stunning tonight, Gayle. Any particular Chinese restaurant you prefer?" "No, you choose" she replied.

Then he proceeded to regale her with another compliment. "Your presence at a hot dog stand with me would have been just fine. As long as I have you all to myself tonight."

The Chinese restaurant he chose had received good reviews. It was but a half hour drive.

When finally seated at the restaurant, they perused the menu. Justin mentioned what he liked. "I love the egg rolls here. I could eat dozens of them. What do you like?"

"If it's spicy, I like it and usually order that from the menu." She looked around. "Do you come here often?"

"Actually, I hate to go out and eat alone, so with Chinese food I order in and get my fill of those things I like."

"Justin, that's foolish. So many people eat out alone. It's the changing times."

He had no response. Instead, he said, "What did you do today?"

She realized that if he did not want to pursue a subject, he simply went on to talk about other things. "Some odds and ends around the house. You?"

"Went out to the school yard and threw some hoops."

Now and again he would say something funny. Gayle would laugh and that eased the conversation between them. They went from subject to subject, and still were able to enjoy their meal.

When they were ready to leave the restaurant, Justin said, "We're not too far from Carlson Point. Want to go there? It has a nice panoramic water view and they have benches where we can sit for a while."

"I like that idea" she said. He took her hand. For Gayle there was such a comfort having a man hold her hand. She liked it.

The area was deserted. While sitting at Carlson Point, they both looked up at the star-filled sky and the crescent moon. "Lovely here, isn't it?" he said softly. "For an artist like you, appreciation for God's handiwork must be great."

"Yes, but we all can appreciate beauty. It is very good for the soul" she smiled.

He replied, "With that irrepressible smile, I have an irrepressible urge." Slowly, he took her in his arms and kissed her. At first, it was a sweet kiss, but then she sensed the change to passion. "Justin, I..." "Sweetie, let me enjoy this. You know I've been waiting some time for this." Gayle closed her eyes and let her emotions control it all. "Oh, Justin, you certainly know how to charm a woman."

"I try" he whispered. "I try."

He kissed and caressed her several times more and she participated with all her sensual energy. "You are quite a woman, Gayle. I'm so glad we met."

When the kissing was over, he continued to hold her, "You know, I don't even have your phone number. Will you let me have it? I'm planning on doing this again."

Gayle brought a bit of levity to his statement. "Are you planning on taking me out again or just planning on kissing me again?"

He moved away from her for a moment. "I like the latter very, very much." Then he pulled her to him.

She snuggled in his arms, "You make me feel so comfortable with your arms around me."

"God, Gayle you are so desirable."

Gayle now felt she needed to go in another direction with him. Everything was happening much too fast. She didn't know if she could handle all this. She had to be honest with him.

"Justin, everything between us is going so fast, I don't know how to respond. I want to say..." Then he was kissing her again in such an ardent fashion. At that moment she realized that is what she wanted. She could not say or do more, nor did she want him to stop.

"You know, I don't even care about your phone number. When I want to see you, I'll just come knocking at your door."

"My dear, don't be rash. Please. There are so many things we have to discuss."

"Like what?"

"I don't even know how old you are."

"Will everything be in order if I were to tell you I am 57 years old?" He stopped and then resumed. "Will that settle everything between us?" She could see he was getting agitated.

A bit startled, she took a deep breath. "Justin, dear, I am 72 years old. Old enough to be your mother."

He did not blink. "I love my mother. Why can't I love you simply as the special woman in my life? Look, Gayle, I don't care about age. All I know is I want you. By your kisses, I see you feel the same way too. Don't blind me with this age stuff."

Gayle was so befuddled. She did not know what arguments to present to him, especially after his last statement. "Justin, can we think this out in a more rational manner?"

"In matters of the heart there is no reasoning, Gayle. None." He stood up. "Let's get going. A baby like me has to be in bed early."

"Now you're being sarcastic, Justin." She stood up too, pulled her shawl across her shoulders and started to walk away. Justin ran after her and grabbed her by the shoulders, turning her around to face him. "Okay, we'll reason this out and with clarity after you—rather, we--think about it. We're both adults. There is nothing wrong with how we feel. Certainly, with how I feel."

As they drove away, nothing was said until they were at her door. "Justin, first thank you for the dinner. Secondly, you know how much I enjoy being with you. Let's think this out and see where it goes. We've had so many talks at the diner, I don't want to spoil anything between us." She opened her door. "Good night, Justin."

For several minutes, he did not respond. Then he said, "Sweetie, I'll see you at the coffee shop on Monday morning." He wanted to kiss her again, but thought better of it. He walked away.

Gayle wanted to continue their Saturday conversation and explain some other things to him. Instead, she suddenly decided to start the new week with something pleasant.

At their next meeting at Dena's Diner, he greeted her as he had in the past. Simply, in a friendly manner.

"Good morning, Gayle." He took the empty chair across from her. He smiled at her and she returned his greeting. There was no one else at the table. He sipped his coffee, as he looked at her over the rim of his cup.

"Justin, I'm going to Cape Cod this Sunday. Some friends are having a get-together."

"And..." he said sadly.

"Some are taking a guest. Would you like to come as my guest? You might enjoy meeting some of them."

What started as a somewhat glum look on his face turned to a half smile. "Are we making up now?"

"You always say the unexpected, Justin."

"Listen, you know I'd love to go with you. Perhaps you can give me some details." As he said that what he was thinking was that she was not closing the door on their friendship.

"It's a late day cocktail hour, or rather hours. I was planning on returning that same night. I'll drive."

"No, no" he said, "I'll be happy to drive in case you imbibe too much."

She looked at him and simply shook her head. "You always throw me off base."

"I know, sweetie."

* * *

The drive to Cape Cod only took them over an hour. Gayle's friends lived right over the Sagamore Bridge. When he had picked her up, he marveled at how stylish she looked. Must be the artist in her, he thought. Gayle had suggested he dress casually and he did. The traffic was not heavy, as most of the autos seemed to be exiting the Cape.

Her friend lived in a lovely cottage about a mile or two from the beach. Justin was at ease meeting her friends. There were artists and musicians and others whose occupation he did not know. After all the introductions, he hooked up with one of the musicians whose tastes in music were pretty similar to his. A guy named Kirk.

As they sipped their drinks, Kirk said, "What are some of the music people you like, Justin?"

"I like people such as the sophisticated Cole Porter. Of course, there's Rodgers and Hammerstein...people of that genre. Lots of great musicals."

"You're a man after my own heart, Justin. I especially like something from 'The Music Man'. You know the beginning, where all the salesmen on the train sing 'You Gotta Know the Territory'. There's a terrific cadence between the men and the movement of the train."

"I thoroughly agree" replied Justin. "Great stuff. A wonderful musical with songs like 'Til There Was You' and the rousing 'Seventy Six Trombones'. Gosh, there are so many more."

And it continued from there. Justin was having a good time. Now and again he would look in Gayle's direction and they would smile at each other. She had been certain he would mingle well.

Justin complimented the hostess, a gal named Norma, on her lovely home, and the great canapes she served. Norma reciprocated by saying she was so glad that Gayle had brought him to her small party. "You must come again, Justin."

When much later Gayle signaled him about leaving, he again thanked Norma. As they drove away, he said "Very nice people and great food." As he looked at her, he said, "Are you tired, sweetie?"

"Past my bedtime, I guess."

"Just sit back and close your eyes. Are you cold?" She shook her head. Not too many miles down the road, he noticed she had fallen asleep. She slept all the way home.

When he arrived at her home, he softly called to her. "Sweetie, you're home."

Startled, she awakened. "Already home?"

"Yes, and you better hurry and get to bed. See you tomorrow." He walked her to her door, as she stifled a yawn. He only kissed her lightly. "Good night."

When they again met at Dena's Diner the next morning, they were smiling at each other. "I think you enjoyed our little trip yesterday."

"Yes" he said. "You have nice friends. An eclectic group, I must say. I didn't thank you last night, so I'm thanking you this morning, Gayle." He took her hand and squeezed it. "Did you sleep well?"

"Yes, I did. Soundly."

"Well, I see that your espresso has made you wide awake."

She nodded. "Do you have a full schedule today, Justin?"

"It's so-so, although you never know what will crop up during the day."

"You know, we have never exchanged telephone numbers. I'll give you mine now and perhaps you can give me yours." She took a note paper from her purse and wrote down her number. "Here you go."

Out of his wallet he took a business card which simply gave his name, address, and telephone number. He handed it to her. "Does this exchange mean I can call you in the middle of the night when I am dreaming of you?"

"I will not reply to that" she said.

Gayle finished her espresso and stood up. "I'm leaving now, Justin, because the light is good for me to paint. Also, I have some errands to do."

"You're not angry about what I just said?"

"Absolutely, not. I'm not angry with you, Justin." She took his hand. "However, I must get going." She smiled at him and stood up and walked out of the restaurant.

Justin finished his coffee and suddenly there was another empty table for the next contingent of people coming in for their fixer upper.

The next few mornings were brief encounters for them, as either he or she had some early morning things to do. Despite their delight in lingering with their cups of coffee, some time there were other matters that needed attending to.

One particular day he was late arriving at the coffee shop. Gayle was not there. He was somewhat angry that he had missed her. Whenever he went there for his morning beverage, it was always with the thought of seeing her. He so looked forward to that. She did not know how she really made his day far more pleasant when they had these encounters.

He moved slowly from the counter to his seat with his coffee. He had missed her. Damn, he said to himself. On the table where they usually sat, he saw that someone had left something behind. When he went to pick it up, he realized it was her booklet of poems, which she often brought with her. She obviously had neglected to pick it up when she had left.

He stood up, placed the cover on his coffee, picked up her booklet, and was hurriedly out the door. It was a short walk to her home. He had a reason now to go there. He rang her doorbell and waited for the door to open. He hoped she was home. Gayle looked surprised to see him.

"Excuse me, sweetie, but I believe you inadvertently left this behind this morning. I guess we missed each other." He handed her the booklet.

"Oh, Justin, how nice of you to return this to me. Do come in."

He stepped over the threshold. Gayle said, "If you can stay a bit, I'll give you another cup of coffee. Come into the kitchen." Justin followed her and looked around as he did so. "Nice home you have here, Gayle."

"Would you like a tour?"

"That would be nice" he replied.

As she moved ahead of him from room to room, she began her litany, "This is the dining room" she gestured with her hand. "This is the living room" she said. Pointing in another direction, she continued, "Back there are two bedrooms." Again gesturing, she said, "That is the kitchen." Then she said, "The house is just large enough for me. I've been living here for several years. It's a nice neighborhood."

All this time, Justin followed her and said the appropriate things, such as "Very nice," "I like this," "Lovely wall color," "Certainly is spacious," etc.

As they walked through the house, she said, "Now, I'll show you my studio."

They walked into a large, well lit room, with much artist's equipment strewn about. Three easels faced him. All he said was, "Hmmm. Isn't it unusual to see three easels set up for an artist?"

"Well, depending on what I have in mind that particular day, then I move to that easel."

Justin's eyes moved from one easel to another. Then his eyes fell on her.

"What do you think of my work?" she asked.

"To one who does not know too much about art, they are all lovely. But you're the loveliest thing in this room." He moved toward her. "I've thought that since the first day I met you." He quickly took her in his arms. Strangely, Gayle did not move, but only looked into his eyes, those desirable eyes. His lips on hers brought out all the long-forgotten passion that a man could draw out of her. And thus began their hunger for each other. "You're very special to me, Gayle." They held on to each other for some time. "Are you shocked at how I feel about you?"

"Honestly," she replied. "No." Then she went on "I think I've been wanting that from you."

"Besides your lovely work, you are the beautiful woman I've been waiting for."

"But, Justin, think of our ages. You're 57 and I'm 72."

"If I were 72 and you were 57 would there be any discussion about this?" His gaze was melting her heart. "I don't ever want to hear that from you. Simply said, you're a woman and I'm the man who wants you."

As she started to speak again, he placed two fingers on her lips. "Don't you dare say a word unless it is that you want me as much as I want you."

Seductively, she smiled and said, "You must be a mind reader."

"Not one more word." He picked her up and went in the direction of her bedroom. Before long they were unleashing their passion for one another. Virtually, the entire day was spent talking, making love, time out for lunch, and back to making love. As the sun began to set, he turned to her breathlessly, "Can I stay here tonight?"

When Gayle threw back her head and laughed, Justin kissed her on the neck. Once more, desire overwhelmed them.

They began doing many things together. Weekdays, it was often coffee; weekends, it would be a special event. One Sunday she suggested the local museum. He agreed.

When they walked into the museum, the first thing they encountered was a large statute of Buddha.

"Wow!" said Justin. "I know one must not laugh at what we are seeing. He may be the real God."

"Justin, really" she admonished him.

"You know that reminds me of something attributed to Buddha. He supposedly said, *'No one saves us but ourselves. No one can and no one may. We ourselves must walk the path'."*

When he finished saying that, he turned to her, grinning. "What do you think, sweetie? Do you want to walk the path of life with me or alone?"

Gayle did not know how to respond. Justin continued, "I think we should live together, Gayle. Considering how we feel about each other, we should be on the same path."

"You've taken me by surprise, Justin."

"Living with you would make me very happy." He smiled at her and gave her a big hug. "Think about it." He took her hand. "C'mon, let's look at the rest of the art treasures there are in here. Isn't that why you took me here today?"

As they walked from gallery to gallery in the museum, Gayle explained the different nuances that each artist brought to his work, but in the back of her mind was his suggestion.

In one of the salons, she stopped dead in her tracks. "Justin, is this a hardship for you?"

"Oh, sweetie, no. Not at all. Please, don't ever think that. I do not enjoy doing this with you. Naturally, I am not as knowledgeable as you about art, but I truly can appreciate what artists and sculptors have done to attain this fame." He took her elbow. "This is a learning lesson for me from a beautiful teacher. However, my idea of living together would please me enormously. Keep explaining things to me and we'll talk about this later. I don't want to spoil our afternoon. Sweetie, look at me." She faced him. "God, you are a work of art yourself."

Gayle smiled at what he had said; then she went on, stopping at certain places and explaining the artist's style, the mode of painting, etc. Still, what he had asked intrigued her.

EPILOGUE

There was knocking on the door. Gayle hurried to answer it. When she finally opened the door, Justin was standing there smiling with one hand behind his back.

"Justin dear," she said. "You have the key here, why are you knocking?"

His smile broadened. He brought his arm forward. He was holding a large bouquet of flowers. He handed them to her. "Here you are, sweetie, happy anniversary."

Perplexed, she replied, "What do you mean?"

"We've been together now for five years. You deserve something for putting up with me all this time. Besides, I love you very much."

Gayle hurriedly moved towards him and touched his hair. "Your hair has some gray in it now." He replied, "I know, sweetie, but yours is still the same light brown color."

Taking the flowers from him, she placed them on a nearby table. Kissing him sweetly, she murmured, "Thank you, dear. Many, many thanks. Loving you makes me feel so young. I love you, Justin." She was crying tears of happiness and remembering what Albert Camus had once said, *"In the depth of winter I finally learned that there was in me an invincible summer."*

Time and years had vanished. They were as equal as a man and woman could be. It was indeed five years of being in each other's lives. Five wonderful years.

"Shall we try for five more years, Gayle?"

She wiped the tears from her face with her fingers, while smiling and nodding. She could not deny herself. His words clutched at her heart. Yes, he was the man for her. He too had never failed to show her how much he loved her.

Then all Justin could say as he hugged her tightly was "Love is a gift. It's ageless."

When the Phone Rings

WHEN THE PHONE RINGS

he day was quite snowy and he was house bound. When the phone rang, Eric was on the other side of the house and not where his landline was. It exasperated him that he could not get there fast enough to answer it, but his injured foot made that difficult. When he was finally able to reach it, without dropping the phone, he shouted into it,

"Hello! Hello!"

"Excuse me, sir, is this..."

"...Who are you looking for?"

"I'm answering the ad for a contractor" the voice on the other end said timidly.

Again shouting, he said, "Yes, this is the place. I placed that ad. What is your name?"

The female voice on the other end said, "My name is Zelia..."

He interrupted, "What sort of a name is Zelia?"

"Sir, that is my first name." His voice was almost intimidating.

His voice softened. "What exactly are you looking to have done?"

"The fences around my property are rather weathered and I need someone to repair and repaint them or perhaps replace them."

"Can you describe them?"

"Well, I don't know how to describe them, but they are about six feet tall and the tops have lattice work on them."

"How long are they?"

"I'd hazard a guess. It's about 25 yards on one side and the same on the other. The back side of the property has hedges."

"I see" said Eric. "Well, it's rather cold these days and I wouldn't want to do an outside job now. Don't you agree? Is it a rush job?"

"No, sir. Quite frankly, it's difficult to find someone to do this type of work. I have tried several companies, but to no avail. If the price is right, I would like you to put me on your list for some time this spring or when the weather is much better. Would you be available, sir?" Zelia was doing her best to sweet talk this individual so he wouldn't brush off her request.

"To begin with I'm dealing with an injured foot and I wouldn't be able to visit your property to give you an estimate or to even look over that which you want done. Also, the weather is abysmal. By the way, do you live far?"

"Well, sir, I live in Rumford, which I believe is about 30 miles away. Your ad indicates Hopkinton as your location." She stopped, "I hear waves in the background, so you must be near the water," said Zelia.

"I must say you have good hearing."

"Sir" she interrupted "can we talk further about your availability."

"You obviously don't have much patience." He stopped, but then continued, "I repeat about my foot…"

"Sir, I'm sorry about your foot, but I really need to know if I can have you look over the work I want done when possible."

"By the way, you have an unusual first name. Are you named for someone in particular?"

"My father was reading a book and liked the name. As you said, it is unusual."

He kept deviating from the subject and Zelia did not know how to get him back on the subject at hand.

He continued, "Also, you have such a sweet voice. How old are you?"

"Sir, I am an adult and I own the property I am referring to."

Then she heard a crash. She heard obscene words emanating from the other end of the phone.

She kept saying, "Hello, hello."

Finally, he was back on the phone, all out of breath. His voice was harsh. "Listen, miss, I just fell off the stool I was sitting on which isn't helping my foot at all. Call me back in a half hour."

"But, sir," she said, "I need to know…." His phone was dead.

All Zelia could think of was that she had probably lost another contact.

All Eric could think of was the pain in his foot and attempting to stand up again. Damn that lady, why did she have to call now. Rushing to answer the phone had brought all this about. Although, his next thought was that he could use the work.

As he had suggested and with great hesitancy, Zelia called back after a half hour had passed.

"Sir, are you all right?"

Diplomatically, he replied, "Zelia, considering how badly things are going today, you're the only good thing I hear."

"Sir…"

"For heaven's sake, will you please call me Eric."

"Eric, is there anything else you need to know about my work request? I'll leave you my phone number."

"Okay, but wait until I find paper and pen."

Zelia heard movement and muttering on the other end, but all she could do was wait for him to return.

"Okay, okay, let's have the number."

Zelia spelled out her number.

Then Eric began expounding on the weather. "Do you have someone to clear your property of snow?"

"Yes, I have a service for snow removal and lawn care in the summer."

"That's good." he said. "Do you live alone?"

"Yes" she replied.

"Are you single?"

"Eric, I simply need someone to do the work I enumerated to you. You don't need the story of my life." She was getting exasperated.

"I know, but you have such an intriguing voice."

Zelia smiled. "Thank you."

"What sort of work do you do?"

"Eric, don't you think you ought to get to bed and perhaps elevate that bad foot?"

"I will, but then I won't be able to talk to you. It's a lonely, dismal day here for me."

"Maybe, you could call some friends?"

"I could, but believe me they don't have the dulcet tone of voice like yours."

Zelia laughed aloud.

"You know I'm even enjoying the sound of your laughter."

He obviously didn't want to hang up and simply wanted to talk further. Zelia thought she would humor him.

"Eric, listen, do you want to tell me about yourself?"

"Okay, I'm a contractor and jack-of-all-trades. So anything you need done, I can probably do it for you. And also, my prices are very reasonable."

"Well, I'm a school teacher. I teach English and because of the snow today, I am at home."

"Interesting" he said.

Then she changed the subject. "Must be nice living near the water?"

"It's great, despite the season. Water is my element. Do you swim?"

"Yes, I do. Like you, I do so enjoy the water."

"You'll have to come down in the summer and perhaps take a swim here."

"Sounds nice" she replied. What else could she say.

"What do you do in your leisure time Zelia?"

"I paint," she replied.

Haughtily, he said, "What do you need me for if you paint?"

"No, no. I paint on canvas."

"Well, how about that." said Eric. "Is there anything in particular you like to paint. Maybe, landscapes or..."

She interrupted, "It varies. Whatever catches my eye."

"Is there a particular artist you especially like?"

"Matisse. Henri Matisse. He lived until 1954. I also like Modigliani. His paintings are easy to identify. The people in them all have elongated faces."

Eric whistled into the phone. "You know your stuff. Why Matisse by the way?"

"I like vibrant colors and he produced some colorful paintings." Then Zelia stopped. "Why are you asking me all these questions?"

"It says a lot about a person if you know what their interests are. Remember what Mahatma Gandhi said, 'If you do nothing, you do nothing'."

On the other end of the phone Zelia smiled at his remark. "Now, about you. What are your interests?"

"Hearing a young woman's enthusiasm."

"Stop that!" she said. Although she was amused at his retort.

He was amused at her supposed anger. "Me. I'm an outdoor person. I like to hunt, fish, and stuff like that."

"Where do you hunt around here?"

"Actually, I go to the north country for hunting. As for fishing, well there is a lot of ocean water around here. So, I fish close to home."

Zelia had nothing else to say, so she now stood up. "Guess, I'll hang up now."

Eric didn't want the conversation to end, so he quickly said, "If I need more information about your project, can I call you back?"

"Of course. I hope things can be done by springtime. Goodbye, for now." She hung up her phone reluctantly.

For Eric a dreary day brought him no one to visit with. The phone was his only contact to the outside world. How lucky to have talked to her for that short period of time. He slowly moved towards his couch. His foot still hurt, so he sat down and happily went over their conversation. How pleasant it had been. Now he had to find a reason to call her back some time soon.

The snow continued. God, he wondered, how many feet was there already on the ground. He had visions of not being able to get out and about for days. Luckily, the larder was well stocked. Unfortunately, he would not be able to use his snow blower because of his foot. Of course, there was always the television as a companion for the day. Other than the news, nothing appealed to him. Under those circumstances, the day would be long. Very long.

There were friends he could have called, but whatever they had to say was simply a rehash of old news. He thought again of Zelia with the sweet voice. Again, he knew he wanted to continue talking to her, but what reason could he use this time. They had never even met.

When Zelia looked out her window the next morning, she saw that there was new fallen snow. This was going to be a big one, she thought. The television announcer was once again rattling off about the storm.

"Look at the bottom of your screen for events that have been cancelled. Also, all schools are closed again today. Stay tuned."

Well, thought Zelia, how was she going to occupy her day now? All her homework had been done and placed in her school folder. Looking over the food in her kitchen, she knew she had enough food provisions for the next few days, as long as the electricity did not go out. Maybe she could do some baking to take up her time. She scurried about her kitchen to see if she had all the ingredients to bake her lemon cake. She had lined up all that was necessary for baking on her counter. Now she looked for an appropriate baking pan. As she did so, her phone rang. She hurried to answer it.

"Hello."

"Zelia, this is Eric." Zelia smiled. "Look, there is something we failed to talk about yesterday. I need to make a certain amount of money for this job."

"What do you mean?" she queried.

"I could make it an hourly arrangement or an overall estimate, despite how long it took me to finish the job."

"Eric, you're the expert in this situation. Whatever you think best. As long as it is not exorbitant. You are still interested in my job, no?"

"Absolutely. Very well, I'll do my best for you after I see what has to be done." Then he stopped talking. When he resumed, he said, "What are you doing today since there are lots of school closings?"

Zelia was curious about his call, but in order to answer him, she said, "I thought I would do some baking."

"Oh, what are you baking?"

"I like most things that are lemon flavored, so I'm making a lemon cake."

"Wow! Sounds great. Bet you're a great baker?"

"Yes, I enjoy baking. Baking is more precise than other types of cooking. You have to follow the recipe exactly as indicated."

Eric was smiling. "Right now you're making me hungry for something baked."

"Eric, don't you have anything to do with yourself today? Maybe read or play some computer game."

"Well, I can't use my snow blower because of my foot and all, so frankly, I really don't know what to do with myself. What you suggested really does not interest me too much. The phone is just about my only contact with the outside world, except for the television."

"What about your friends?"

"I'm all talked out with them."

When he first called, Zelia couldn't understand why he had called her with such an obviously unimportant question about the cost for the work. He hadn't even seen her property yet.

He must have deduced what she was thinking. "Hope you don't mind my calling you this morning?"

"No, no, not at all."

"Frankly, I just wanted to hear your voice again."

Zelia smiled as she played with the telephone cord. "Thank you. A nice thing for you to say."

"I don't mean to be impertinent, but how old are you?"

Then Zelia laughed. "I know most women don't want to answer that question, but I'll be honest with you. I am 25 years old. And you?"

"I'm 27" he said.

"Well, that's settled" she replied. "Do you want to know how tall I am?"

"No, no. I hope you're not angry with me?"

"Eric, it's hardly something to be angry about."

"Good." He hesitated. "Right now I'm salivating at the thought of some lemon cake."

"You know what I'll do. When it's done, I'll send you a piece by drone. How's that?"

Eric laughed heartily. "You sure know how to let a guy feel good on such a dreary day."

When they both had stopped laughing, he said seriously, "Tell me about yourself, Zelia."

Zelia figured she would humor him. On such a day, most people alone, like themselves, needed to talk with someone in order to make the long day hurry by. They had not yet met and still there was a coziness about talking to each other.

She was thinking about what she could converse with him about.

"I have traveled to Europe" she said.

"Sounds absolutely great. Tell me all about it." He sat down to hear it all.

"After I graduated college, my folks treated me to a two-week trip to Europe, specifically, Paris and Rome. Paris, of course, with its Eiffel Tower, is something to behold. I couldn't believe I was in such a place; a place I had often seen in pictures. It is a magic city. The Arc de Triomph, the Champs Elysees. Then I got on a bateau mouche—that's the boat that travels up and down the River Seine. Everything was delightful. Of course, the bistros always brought out my hunger with all the simple but elegant goodies on their menus. People walking to their homes with baguettes under their arms. You know what baguettes are?"

"Yes" he replied, as he listened to the enthusiasm in her voice. What a mellifluous voice.

She continued, "There was so much to see. Fortunately, my camera enabled me to relive the places I had seen once I returned home. Then I went on to Rome. Of course, we all know about the Coliseum." As an aside, she said, "There are lots of cats there." Then she resumed where she had left off. "The many buildings with architectural splendor. Then the Vatican and all its statuary, especially the well-known Pietá. To my eyes it was all incredible. The art really uplifted my soul. To see what was put on canvas long ago. All of it was awe-inspiring. That's why I picked up my brush and my canvas when I came home. In a hundred years I could never duplicate those treasures. Then, there was..."

Eric quietly interrupted her. "You have no idea what your descriptions are doing to my ear." Spontaneously, he said, "You must be a beautiful woman, Zelia. I can't recall when I last heard someone talk to me with such heartful feeling."

There was no response on the other end of the phone. "Zelia, Zelia, are you there?"

Softly he heard her breathe into the phone, "Thank you, Eric. You are so kind. Sometimes, I get emotional about the beautiful and wondrous things I've seen."

"Considering that we have never met, I'm terribly impressed talking and listening to you. I'm truly looking forward to meeting you...soon."

Not knowing what else to say, Zelia stood up straight. She had to say something to end the conversation now. "Eric, I must go." She looked at what she had assembled for her cake baking. "Eric, the butter is melting." Then she quietly hung up.

Eric was crestfallen. It had been going so beautifully, then it stopped. He hobbled over to the television, clicked the remote, and just sat there listening to an unknown voice and shaking his head.

* * *

It was running into the weekend and Zelia knew that the next two days would probably be long ones since the snow mounds outside her home made it difficult for her to go out. She was happy that her lemon cake had turned out so well. Although she admired it, she had not yet cut it or tasted it. She decided a little music would cheer her up. Looking at her many CD's, she sought one that was uplifting. Finally, she chose one. It was a classical guitarist playing the most soulful Spanish music. That was it. Maybe not quite uplifting, but it suited her mood.

She had talked to a couple of friends on the phone, but it was pretty much what had been said several times before. Most of what was discussed did not heartened her, but at least it was other voices. She began thinking what Eric was doing with his injured leg. It occurred to her that she had not given him her address. Should she call him? Certainly, she had enjoyed their other conversations. Yes or no? As she hummed along with the music, she realized there was nothing to lose. She had a valid reason.

The phone rang at Eric's home. It rang several times. Maybe, he had gone out after all, she thought. Suddenly, he picked up. "Hello, hello, hello?"

"Eric, I hope I did not disturb you?"

"Zelia? No, not at all." He was smiling. "I was making myself a sandwich in the kitchen. My landline is in the living room and it takes me a bit of time to reach it. Is something wrong?"

"I realized I had neglected to give you my address."

"That's certainly most important. But right now, not a problem. We have time. Have to wait for this snow to melt away, you know."

She thought she would bring a little levity into her talk with him. "Also, I want you to know that a slice of my lemon cake will soon be arriving at your house by drone."

Eric could do nothing else but laugh when she said that. "Okay, I'll be on the lookout for it." Then he turned serious. "What are you doing now?"

"I decided some music was just what I needed today. I'm listening to a guitarist playing Spanish music."

"Really? Would you believe me if I told you I play the guitar?"

"You're joking."

"Honestly. There's a small cafe not too far from my home called Amanda's Cafe. On weekends I have a gig there, along with some other guys I know."

"What do you play?"

"Mostly, country music, but sometimes we also play pop for the audience."

"How incredible that we both like guitar music, although mine is rather different from yours."

"How about that" he said.

He paused. "What else do we have in common?"

Meekly, she replied, "I have no idea."

Nothing else was said for several minutes. "Zelia, are you still there?"

"Yes, I'm here."

Eric thought fast. What else could he say to her now? "How will you spend the rest of the day?"

"I have no idea. I'm constrained being in the house all day. I hope my snow removal service can get here before school resumes Monday."

"If not, I'll have to get on that drone and shoot over to your place to remove the snow by your house."

More laughter.

"Seriously, I hope I can meet you soon" he said in the most heartfelt way.

"That would be nice," she whispered.

"Instead of waiting for the good weather to check out your fences, I'll make it a point to visit with you before that. Maybe as soon as they clear the roads."

"Yes" she said sweetly "I would like that very much."

"Okay, it's a date. We have that settled." Wonderful, he thought, he would finally meet her. Now for her address.

"Oh, my, yes, give me your address." His pen and paper were at hand.

Zelia slowly gave him her address, listening as he went over it again with her. He absolutely did not want to get this one wrong.

* * *

When Zelia's doorbell rang, she hurried to answer it. She already knew who would be on the other side. She stopped, took a deep breath, and then opened the door.

An attractive man confronted her. "If you are not Eric, you have the wrong house."

He smiled and quietly said, "By that sweet voice I know I have the right house. I have not made a mistake." Continuing, he said,

"Lovely Zelia. At last." He took her hand and kissed it. She was flustered, but was able to say, "Come in, Eric." She stepped aside.

Certainly, they both probably had the same thought as he entered the house. Talk about work on the fences, well that would come later. They had already discussed it all by phone. Now by far was the best part. As the door closed behind them, they would soon be learning much more about each other. In person.

Dream with Me

DREAM WITH ME

nnalee and Lyle had been married 49 years and had always dreamed of a special something they would do for their 50th wedding anniversary. A month's cruise to the Orient or perhaps traveling around the Mediterranean. What a pleasant dream it had been for some time. However, it was not to be. Lyle died just months before their 50th year together as man and wife. Three years of trips to the cancer clinic had not resolved the terrible lingering illness that plagued him. As Annalee often said, "Much too soon."

But, of course, after so many years together they could almost read each other's thoughts. It was natural that for many nights she would dream of him. She prayed that he was now in a peaceful place, free of pain and suffering. Oh, but how she missed him.

She would often look around their bedroom where on many occasions events of the day caused them to laugh. Then there were situations where she would cry about something, while Lyle consoled her and reminded her that nothing was gained by crying. He would hug her and allay her fears. The best moments were when they joined together in all the sweetness and passion that was theirs alone. It confirmed the great love they had for each other. Lyle would say the stars aligned and they were meant to be together.

Some things they had gathered in their travels were also in their bedroom. Annalee looked over at the dreamcatcher they had found when they had traveled west to the Great Plains. Legend was that only good dreams would pass through the center hole to the sleeping person, while bad dreams were trapped and died. Annalee often smiled and hoped it was true.

When she took to her bed at nighttime, she would pick up a book and read until sleep overtook her. Comforting, but lonely. Sometimes, she would put her book down and talk to Lyle as if he were present. No response was ever forthcoming, but that was to be expected. No one from the afterlife ever returned to converse with their loved ones. Except, one night as she was starting to fall asleep, she heard that familiar voice.

"Annalee, Annalee, how are you, my love? I do so miss you."

"I'd like so much to meet with you and talk, as we did in the past. Can you meet me at the corner of 7th and 8th Avenues, by the beach? I'll be looking for you at 7 a.m."

Annalee had often gone walking in that area and knew it well. "Yes, yes" she replied. "I'll be there. Will you really be there?"

"I'll be there, my love."

Annalee mulled over what she had heard. Was this possible? She had to subsist on so many memories. This caused her to cry. As Lyle had often said nothing came of crying. Should she go to the beach to see if Lyle was really there? Then again, what did she have to lose. She walked on the beach daily. Thinking and re-thinking it all, she decided she would go in the morning.

With great anticipation she drove down to the beach early the next day. She walked to the well-known spot, although it was still a bit foggy for such an early hour. There was a barrier between 7th and 8th Avenue, something comparable to a berm. She waited, looking around for Lyle to appear.

Suddenly, out of the fog appeared Lyle. She could not believe it. It simply was not possible. Lyle, her Lyle, with a big smile on his face, walking toward her. He stopped at a given point on one side of the barrier.

"Good morning, my love. Even in the early morning you are still my beautiful Annalee."

Annalee gasped, with her hand to her mouth, she cried out his name, "Lyle, my Lyle. Oh, darling, it is so good to see you."

As she tried to get over the barrier, Lyle stopped her. *"My love, please understand, we can only stay at this distance, but still talk." Hesitating, he continued, "Do you recall when we first met? I was hurrying to my classes and you were rushing from the other side. Then you stumbled, with your books strewed all around. I had to stop and help. As I proceeded to pick up your books, you admonished me for getting in your way as you rushed to class. I was flabbergasted. Here I was trying to be a gentleman. Instead you were getting angry with me and blaming me for your fall."*

Lyle then started to laugh. Annalee also began to laugh, remembering it all. Then she started in by continuing, "I said something about your getting in my way. But you slyly smiled at me and said, 'If this is the way I get to meet a beautiful girl like you, well then I'll make it a point to always get in your way.' Then we stopped for a moment and began to laugh. Remember?"

Lyle nodded his head over and over. Once she had begun, Annalee continued. It was so wonderful to reminisce. "And, Lyle, do you remember when we got married, how it rained despite being the month of June? My flowers all drooped, yet we held hands tightly and laughed. When we got into the limousine taking us to our reception, the laughter brought out the romantic in you and you kissed me continually until I said, 'There won't be any kisses left over for later.' Then you replied, 'Oh, yes, there will. Trust me, there'll be more of everything'." Again, Lyle laughed, as he too remembered.

Lyle then picked up the conversation, *"Do you recall when we furnished our new home, we went to so many places looking for pieces for our home that also were economical. It was exhausting, but such fun. Don't you agree?"*

Annalee began to relax as they continued to talk, both laughing at the experiences they had in their lives which no one could understand or enjoy but they themselves.

The sun was beginning to get brighter and the fog was beginning to dissipate.

"Annalee, my love, I must leave now. Can we meet again tomorrow at this time?"

"Darling" she argued. "No, don't leave me just yet. Please" she pleaded. The fog was lifting and Lyle was gone. Annalee sat alone and cried. After a period of time she knew she had to move away from this spot and walk back to where she had come from. He had said tomorrow. Yes, yes, tomorrow.

Once home, she made herself breakfast and went out to the clubhouse of the complex where she lived. The others were there and simply asked if she had taken her morning walk. She replied that she had and continued with the others in conversation.

One of her friends, Rose, noticed that Annalee seemed preoccupied. "Is everything all right?" she asked.

Sadly, Annalee answered, "Oh, yes, just a bit tired." In order to change the mood, she continued, "Are we going to the Christian Women's luncheon today?"

Rose looked up, "I didn't buy that new outfit for nothing. Remember, the Ritz Carleton is a pretty fancy place. By the way, do you want to ride with me?"

"Great, yes" replied Annalee. "See you at 11:30." The hour for their luncheon dates was invariably the same.

Once in her apartment, Annalee once again thought about her encounter with Lyle. Lyle, the love of her life. She was confused, but she had to see him again tomorrow so that he could explain what their meetings were all about.

She then went to her closet and picked an outfit for her luncheon date. The day could be quite long without something to do. It was the bane of a widow's existence.

The next morning she was awake earlier than usual. She was anxious to see Lyle again and talk to him as they had done over their many years together. Once dressed, she was out the door. Rose was already outdoors. "Want some company on your walk, Annalee?" "Not today, I have an errand," said Annalee. The last thing she needed was Rose beside her this morning.

When she got to the beach, the fog was hovering over the beach. She went to the spot Lyle had chosen. She did not want to be late, so she hurried. She almost fell as it was difficult traipsing on the sand.

Then she saw him coming out of the fog.

"Annalee, my love. Good day to you, lovely woman. Over the years I always told you that you got more beautiful."

"Oh, Lyle, you flatterer." Then she remembered something from their past. "Do you recall when we went to the French Riviera and you saw several young ladies going topless at the beach? I recall how you reacted that day"

Lyle laughed. *"I was flabbergasted seeing those nubile girls with their breasts exposed. Why, here we are so puritanical you would never see that. Although, like any man they were lovely to look at."*

"Yes, but when you said you wanted to take pictures of them, I thought I would suffer from an apoplectic fit," Annalee said. Together they laughed again, rethinking it all.

The laughing continued as they remembered other humorous things that had occurred over the years.

As the sun was beginning to come up, the fog lifted and Lyle said sadly, *"Tomorrow, my love. Tomorrow."*

Although Annalee wanted to prolong their conversation, she knew it would not happen. He was gone.

Annalee returned to her apartment, always a bit forlorn. However, she knew sometime soon she and her friends would be playing tennis. She now had to pick up her mail. Although, as she thought again of her morning encounters with Lyle, she could not help but smile.

The next day she also remembered that she had to see her doctor for the usual checkup. True, she had been slowing down, but seeing Lyle had invigorated her somewhat. What a wonderful man she had married. Oh, how she missed being with him. It wasn't fair that somehow women outlived their spouses, leaving such an emptiness in their lives. Friends were great, but somehow they could not provide the intimacy between husband and wife, as well as all those things that were only said within the confines of their relationship.

The following morning she again went to meet Lyle and they reminisced about so many things. Too soon at sunup he was gone.

When she returned home, she readied for her doctor's appointment. Once there, he checked her out thoroughly. However, he did indicate that she looked tired. "Are you resting enough without overdoing it?" he said. "As best I can, given my age" she replied. "Well" he said, "rest more and take some vitamins."

The days continued with the same routine. She would be at the beach at the prescribed time and Lyle would meet her at the barrier. They would talk and talk until the fog lifted. She would return home enervated and continue with her daily routine.

Another day when Lyle and Annalee were talking she told him the association where she lived was having a dinner dance at the club house. "I hesitate about going. There are so many women and so few men" she said. "All I end up doing is tapping my feet when the dancing starts."

Lyle encouraged her to attend. *"My love, go and enjoy yourself a bit. I don't want you sitting alone in your apartment. I won't be your dance partner, but it will be a diversion for you."* Annalee listened to him and finally agreed to his suggestion. Then she recalled a humorous incident that had occurred some years back when they were together at another dinner dance.

"Darling, do you remember that dinner dance we attended and how you danced with me and the two widows at our table?" Lyle nodded. Annalee continued, "The funniest part was when someone stopped me the following day and asked if my partner was single. They were talking about you. All those ladies who were alone and had observed you wanted to meet you and either get your phone number or give you theirs."

Suddenly, they were both laughing heartily. *"Of course, I could have been pretty popular if I was alone"* said Lyle. Annalee quickly responded, "I would never have allowed that. You were always mine." Lyle's comeback was, *"I never looked at another woman. You were always my love."* With her eyes downcast, she replied, "I know."

As always, the fog began to lift and those treasured moments ended for the day.

When Annalee returned home, she went to her mailbox for her mail. She looked everything over and decided to go home and make out some checks, a monthly chore. There was also a current magazine for her to spend some time with.

When she awakened one morning, Annalee felt very tired. She looked at her bedside clock. She did a double take. It was later than usual. She had to hurry to the beach. She did not want to miss meeting Lyle. She gathered her clothes, was out the door in a hurry, and motoring down to the beach faster than usual.

Upon arriving, she ran to their assigned spot. She was all out of breath. It was still foggy, but he was there waiting for her. *"What's the matter, my love?"* "I'm sorry, darling, I overslept. I've been so tired lately." *"Annalee, please take it slow."* "I didn't want to miss seeing you, darling." *"Never a problem, my love."*

Suddenly, she felt quite dizzy and collapsed by the barrier where he stood. Someone in the distance was yelling, "A lady has fallen down on the beach and is not getting up. Call an ambulance."

But it really was not necessary. Lyle came across the barrier. This time he picked her up and took her by the hand. *"Come with me, my love. Come with me."* The fog had lifted.

Love You Much

LOVE YOU MUCH

llen looked out the airport window at the plane which she soon would be boarding for her return home. The airline employee behind the counter was calling the seat numbers. Ellen looked around as she waited for hers to be announced. As each number was called, people were filing into the aircraft.

Across the large lounge area she also noticed the other airlines that had arrived, as well as the people who were disembarking. Most everyone was happy to have reached their destination. Those that awaited them looked with anticipation for the next person to step into the lounge.

Then she saw him. Quickly he rushed to greet several people coming into view. She stopped dead in her tracks and noticed the greetings that followed. He hugged and kissed each of them, and there were smiles on all sides. Ellen took it all in and began remembering what had happened just two months ago. Her eyes were teary. The decision had extracted a heavy price from her. A necessary price.

* * *

The local playhouse was having a musical production. Being alone in this new town, Ellen called the number she had seen listed in the local newspaper. She asked about the availability of one seat for the Saturday matinee. The person on the phone said yes, they did have one seat. Ellen chose among the seats that were available, gave them her credit card number, and asked that they hold same for her arrival. Going to the theater alone was not something she ordinarily did, but being in this town to work for a couple of months, there was no one she knew well enough to invite.

The day of the performance started out cloudy. By the time she had left her hotel for the theater, which was in walking distance, the rain was coming down heavily. She was well dressed in all of her rain gear. After arriving at the theater, she disengaged herself of her outer clothing. Since the seat adjacent to hers was empty, she placed that clothing next to her. A gentleman sitting on the other side of the empty seat smiled as she maneuvered to get everything in place so she could enjoy the show.

"Is this empty seat for someone you are awaiting?"

"No" said he "I'm alone." Then he added "You know you could have put your outer clothing where they check coats."

"Heavens" she said "I did not think of that. Being from out of town is no excuse, but I came in hurriedly and... here I am." She tried smiling at him. "I hope my paraphernalia does not disturb you."

Again he smiled: "No, no. Not at all."

All then became quiet as the houselights dimmed and the show began.

At intermission she did not arise from her seat, while others did. Upon his return, the same man said, "You should have gotten up to take a breather."

"I know" she said, "but... I simply didn't."

"You said you were from out of town. What are you doing here?" He was making small talk.

"My company sent me here for a couple of months to check and meet with the personnel who distribute our products. I work for a pharmaceutical company." She stopped a moment and then resumed. "I've never been here before. Although, I'm often pleasantly surprised by becoming acquainted with new places." She stopped again. "Are you a native of this town?"

"Yes, I'm an attorney here. We are presently handling a big case which requires immediate attention. I won't be able to vacation during these summer months. We're dealing with time constraints."

"My, that's too bad. From the little I've seen this seems like a really nice part of the country."

Continuing, he said: "Our beaches and seashore are some of the best you'll find anywhere. And remember, I do not work for the Chamber of Commerce."

They both laughed. He held out his hand. "I'm Alex."

She took his hand and replied, "I'm Ellen."

The orchestra started anew, indicating that intermission was over.

"Enjoy the rest of the show," he said, as the house lights again dimmed.

The next hour and one half passed swiftly with most everyone in rapt attention. When the show concluded, everyone began their departures.

As Alex arose, he took out his wallet and handed her his card. "If you need a lawyer while you are here, you can call me."

"Thank you. But what I need now is the name of some good eating places. Can you recommend any?"

"Oh, there are many nearby. Tell you what, if you are amenable, there is a great Mediterranean restaurant within walking distance "I'm eating alone. Perhaps you can join me." He looked at her, awaiting her response. "Am I being too forward?"

"Oh, no, you're being very kind with your offer" She hesitated. "That's fine with me."

Now that they had introduced themselves, he helped her with her rain gear. "If you come along with me, I'll pick up my coat and we can be on our way; it's just a very short distance."

Outdoors, the rain had abated. As they walked along, she picked up the conversation. "Have you lived here long?"

"All my life. I've had opportunities elsewhere, but I just didn't want to uproot myself. What about you?"

"Well, as I said before, I've had this job for several years. I travel around the country, staying a month or two in a new city to check out the personnel and their distribution of our products. Sometimes it's fun and sometimes it gets weary. However, all in all, I do enjoy it. I am single and can do this without a great disruption in my life."

"I guess if you enjoy it, that's the key to everything" he said. "I have a family here and I can't disrupt their lives."

"Oh, how nice. A large family?"

"I have a wife, twin girls and a young son."

"Must keep you busy?"

"And necessitating my working hard" Alex replied with a grin. They had arrived at the restaurant and he said, "Here we go."

The restaurant fortunately was not crowded so that their wait for a table was brief. When they were seated, the waiter handed them the menu.

"The food here is quite good" said Alex. "I come here often."

They perused the menu and made their choices. "Would you like some wine with your meal?" asked Alex.

"Sounds good. I'll have Chablis."

Turning to the waiter, he said, "Waiter, two glasses of Chablis wine."

As they enjoyed their meal, each found the other interesting and quite knowledgeable about many things. Ellen told him of the places where she had been sent. "Some good; others, not" she grimaced.

Alex enjoyed how animated she would get. He, too, had some amusing legal stories to tell. They were conversing like old friends.

When they finally left the restaurant, he said "I'll be happy to walk you to your hotel."

"Why, thank you, Alex. I'm staying at the Hotel Bristol."

Ellen's hotel was a short distance away. When they arrived, he said, "If you need anything or want to know what attractions there are hereabouts, well, you have my card." He stopped and faced her directly, "Ellen, you've been a delightful dinner companion."

Again, she thanked him. She walked away, but turned once more to wave to him. He blew her a kiss. She was surprised, but decided to think nothing of it. Once ensconced in her hotel room, she took off her shoes and lay down on the bed. Such a nice day, she thought.

The following day was a Sunday and again it was raining. She decided to stay put in her hotel room and go over her work load for the upcoming week.

The week began with Ellen renting an automobile with the necessary GPS for her scheduled visits around the city. It was always the same routine, introducing herself at the different offices, and then going on with the necessary queries, etc. At the end of the day she returned to her hotel, took a shower, and then arranged to have her evening meal in the hotel dining room.

Subsequent days brought more of the same. She got along well with the employees she met, most of whom were kind and answered all her questions. All the encounters she had went well. However, no one asked her to join them in whatever they were doing socially. That was par for the course. She inquired of the concierge at the hotel about things to do in town. He was most helpful and also gave her some pamphlets. And she found herself thinking of things to do to fill up her time while here. Perhaps, enjoying the museums, the city park, the boats sailing at the river front, and perhaps discovering interesting shops. She smiled. There was always shopping. Somehow, she would fill up her days and her off-work time. There was also the city library to visit and see if there were other things she could pursue. It was pretty much what she had done time and time again.

After being in this new town for a couple of weeks, Ellen mulled over what to do now with her free time. When she returned to her hotel after her last appointment on Friday evening, her phone rang. Upon answering it, she heard Alex's voice saying, "How is the stranger in our town doing?"

Surprised, she replied, "Alex, how nice to hear from you." Her first thoughts were that hearing a familiar voice in a strange town was comforting. "How is your work load going?"

"Ellen, don't ask. There's still much to be done. How tiresome it can be. However, I need a break this weekend. I had a thought. There will be a local art festival, which you might enjoy. Would you be interested? Perhaps, I could pick you up Sunday morning. We could have breakfast, and then walk to the festival. How does that sound?"

Of his invitation, Ellen thought it could be something pleasant to do. "I'm amenable to your suggestion. Can you give me some details?"

"Well," said he, "I know a great restaurant which makes the best Eggs Benedict. Do you like Eggs Benedict?"

Happily, she said, "I love them. They are usually my first choice when I go out to breakfast."

"Okay, I'll pick you up Sunday about 10 a.m. Afterwards, we'll walk to the festival. Listen, wear flat shoes since there's a lot of walking to do. Does that appeal to you?"

Ellen replied, "Yes, indeed. Thanks for your kind invitation. I look forward to Sunday."

After hanging up, Ellen thought of his call. She had found him to be an interesting man with whom she was completely at ease, although he was married. She looked at the invitation as spending a few hours with a new friend.

When he saw her on Sunday, he said, "You're a better choice than those dull law books. I certainly have a big work load still ahead of me, but luckily the weekends are mine."

After a hearty breakfast, which Ellen thoroughly enjoyed, they walked away completely satisfied. Ellen turned to Alex, "You were right. The breakfast was wonderful. You make great choices for this out-of-towner."

The art festival was not far away. Artists from all over the country were represented. Ellen enjoyed the great assortment of various modes of work presented by these people. While surveying some art work in one of the stalls, her eyes fell upon a painting on glass which appealed to her. "Alex, what do you think?" she asked. "I like it" he said approvingly. When she bought it, he took it from her and carried it for her.

As the day was ending, Alex suggested sitting by the shore near the city park. Silently, they spent a little time watching the graceful sailboats go by.

Upon returning to her hotel, Alex asked if she wanted something to eat. Ellen declined, but thanked him for a pleasant day. "Gosh," she said, "we've talked about virtually everything under the sun." Alex smiled at her statement. In the hotel lobby, he said good night and said quietly, "I truly enjoy being with you, Ellen." As he walked away, he turned and blew her a kiss.

* * *

As time went on, Alex would call her now and again or take her out on a Sunday for a few hours. He told her his family was vacationing in Michigan. Sometimes, he would even call her at the conclusion of her work day. Ellen realized she not only looked forward to hearing from him, but also would only admit to herself that she liked this man more and more. She was certain he felt the same way too. There was a mutual loneliness that seemed to make them good company for each other, They were simpatico. However, the dilemma of his being a married man troubled her.

The upcoming weekend was a three-day one. Ellen thought the seashore for a few days would be great. Bed and breakfast establishments appealed to her, but she was not acquainted with the local ones. She went to her computer and scrolled bed and breakfasts nearby. There were many with good reviews. She had to make a decision, but then she had a thought. She would call Alex as he knew the territory well and could possibly be helpful with her choice.

His business card was in her wallet. She pulled it out and called his office. She identified herself to the operator. After a couple of minutes she heard, "What a very nice surprise, Ellen. How's your work going? Tell me, are you still enjoying our great city? I told you we have a great city here."

She replied, "Surely, you must work for the local Chamber of Commerce?"

Alex laughed. "No, no." He hesitated. "What can I do for you?"

"Well, since you know this area so well, could you recommend a bed and breakfast by the seashore? That's what I'm planning for this long weekend."

"I have just the place. It's called Brad's Bed and Breakfast. They also serve lunch and dinner. It's only an hour's drive from here. You could walk out the back door and in a matter of minutes be swimming. It's a nice place and I believe you would enjoy it. You have a GPS on your car?" When she replied yes, he continued, "I would recommend it highly." He stopped for a moment. "Listen, I am very busy now. Let me know how you make out. We'll talk soon."

Ellen hurriedly thanked him. She then went to her computer and got the necessary information regarding address and phone number. She called and made a reservation, telling them she would be arriving late on Friday afternoon.

The drive to her destination was pleasant, but it was stop and go because others obviously had similar plans. Upon arrival, she registered, received information as to meals and local activities, and was given a lovely bedroom at the back of the house. Out its window she saw the water sloshing across the rock wall adjacent to the property. How soothing the water was, she thought.

The next morning she put on her bathing suit with a cover-up and went in to breakfast. Two other couples were there. She greeted them and introduced herself. One young couple was from upstate New York, while the other couple came from Philadelphia.

The owners had prepared a luscious selection for the morning meal, enough to take good care of the taste buds. There was juice, a large quiche, scrambled eggs, bacon, blueberry muffins, French toast, and large carafes full of coffee, all of which made for a hearty breakfast. When finished, she said to one and all, "Have a good day." Off she went to the nearby beach. It was secluded. With no one around Ellen placed her beach blanket and towel (all provided by the inn) on the ground and went in for a swim. After sunbathing for an hour more, she picked up her things, returned to her room, removed her wet suit, hung it out to dry, and took a refreshing shower. Resting for an hour more on her bed, she thought she would explore this quaint town. Dressed in a T-shirt, shorts and flats, she soon was out the door.

Walking hurriedly down the front steps, Ellen did a double take. Exiting from a car nearby was Alex, dressed in casual attire. Was that really Alex? He looked up as she came down the stairs. They stared at one another. Ellen was the first to speak. "Whatever are you doing here?"

Alex sounded somewhat irritable as he answered her. "Listen, all that material for our big case was getting to me. Hardly the weekend to be stuck in an office with onerous law books. I thought getting away and perhaps seeing you again would be just the thing for me. I need someone to talk to, not those stuffy tomes."

Ellen laughed at his explanation, "Makes sense to me."

His voice softened then. "I'll probably see you later."

She put on her sunglasses and waved as she went on her way. But he had said, "Perhaps seeing you again would be just the thing for me." A married man saying that to her was rather surprising, but he probably meant it only in a friendly way.

Her walk into town proved great fun. She bought herself a printed sundress, some new flats, and a straw hat, which she quickly placed on her head. To remind herself of her stay here, she also bought a couple of souvenirs. Leisurely, she walked along several streets, enjoying them all after her work week. It was early afternoon when she returned to the inn. Peeking in the dining room, she saw Alex sitting there drinking a cold beverage.

He looked up. "The lady looks lovely in her straw hat. I was hoping to have lunch with you."

"Sorry," she said, "but since this is my first visit here, I dawdled and bought some things." She removed her hat.

He smiled at her. "If you like, we can lunch now as the buffet table is still set up." She placed her things on an adjacent chair and followed him to the buffet table, where each made food choices.

"Are you going to relax now that you're away from your office?"

"With a lovely woman to talk to, I'll do my best."

Ellen changed the subject. Looking around the room, she gestured with her hands. "Thanks. This was a great choice you made for me." Then she decided to pursue neutral subjects as they ate. This allowed her to be more at ease with him.

"What will you do the rest of the afternoon?" he asked.

"I really hadn't given it much thought."

"What say I rent a boat and we row across the water to see the two or three islands out there?"

He saw her enthusiasm. "Sounds like fun" she said. "However, I want to pay my share for the rental." His reply was, "Absolutely not."

After lunch, they walked together to the riverfront where Alex rented a small boat. He helped her in and soon they were pushing out to sea. Ellen had her straw hat on again.

"This little island we are heading to is called Blueberry Island because a lot of wild berries grow there."

Ellen said little, but took it all in. There was nothing like the tranquility of the water as it splashed around them. She simply said, "Lovely."

Alex looked directly at her. "Lovely indeed." She looked down and said no more.

Then he began telling her the history of the town, the islands, and the surrounding area. For a first-time visitor, Ellen was enjoying it all.

When they finally returned to the dock, he took her hand and helped her out of the boat. He was pulling her close to him. She said nothing. She did not know if it was inadvertent or not. "C'mon, let's walk back," he said. Still holding her hand, he suggested a drink at one of the bars they saw en route.

She followed him to a place called appropriately, The Town Tap. "Will we miss supper, Alex?"

"Don't worry, he said. "The dining room is opened late."

The Town Tap had a music combo that was playing. When the waiter came, Alex said, "Can I order for you, Ellen?" She nodded, as she removed her hat and sat down at a little table. He did not sit down, but took her hand. "Let's dance." He walked her to the dance floor and took her in his arms.

Suddenly, she felt a strange thrill being held this way by him. Alex must have read her mind, as he whispered, "I like the feel of you."

Ellen tried to collect her thoughts and innocuously said instead, "Are you missing your family?"

"Yes... but I still like the feel of you," he said as they continued to dance.

For their brief stay there, they made idle chatter. Alex asked her the usual question, "Why is a lovely woman like you not married?"

Ellen answered, "Well, I do have a long-standing beau named Robert. I am very fond of him and sometimes we talk marriage."

All Alex could say was, "I see."

Suddenly, Ellen felt an electricity between them, as he placed his hand over hers. Although she pulled her hand away, they continued drinking. Alex looked at her and said nothing. She did not know how to handle what seemed to be happening. Everything felt right, but also wrong. Finally, sensing her uneasiness, he said, "Shall we go?"

Quickly, she rose from her chair and said quietly, "Yes."

As they walked back to the inn, Ellen enjoyed the view around her, while Alex said nothing. Once there, the others were already having their evening meal. Alex and Ellen joined them, after making their meal choices.

The young couple named Nancy and Jeff from upstate New York began the conversation. Suddenly, Nancy said, "Anyone want to play Scrabble after dinner?" Ellen quickly replied, "Oh, I love that game. I'm in." They looked to Alex, but he shook his head. "I'm going to retire early." After his meal, he said good night to everyone and left the dining room.

Nancy turned to Ellen and asked, "Is he your boyfriend?" "Oh, no, since I'm on a work assignment and from out of town, I met him when I got here. When I told him I needed suggestions on bed and breakfast spots, he mentioned this place. So that's how I find myself here." She smiled, "It's a great spot, isn't it?" Nancy agreed. "Now, tell me about both of you," continued Ellen.

Nancy turned to Jeff and took his hand. "Well, this happens to be the one-year anniversary of our marriage and we wanted to celebrate somewhere special. Like you, we think this is a real nice place."

Smiling, Ellen lifted her glass in their direction, saying, "I wish you both a lifetime of happiness."

With enthusiasm they began to play Scrabble. Nancy especially was an eager player. Both Jeff and Ellen looked at her as she scrutinized her tiles and the board. Then she suddenly sat up, placed her tiles in the proper place, and shouted, "I have a word. 'Ennui'." She looked from one to the other, gloating, while the other two laughed at her. The tone for the game had been set and that's how it continued until they concluded the game.

"Listen, have you two gone into the water yet or are you still in honeymoon mode?" said Ellen. When they all laughed, Ellen continued, "Okay, tomorrow morning after breakfast get your towels and stuff. We'll meet for a swim. How does that sound?" Ellen began thinking how pleasant this day had been.

When at evening's end they finally adjourned, Jeff said, "That game was fun. I'll be sleeping with this big winner." He pointed to his wife and laughingly, took her hand. "See you in the morning, Ellen."

The next morning when Ellen checked the weather for that day, she heard what she wanted to hear on television. Sunny and warm.

When Ellen arrived at the water's edge she placed her straw hat by her side. The lovebirds were already there. How caring they were of each other, Ellen thought. The blush of a new life together had not worn off on them.

Jeff looked out at the water. "Gosh, that water looks great." He turned to the two women, "Shall we?" All three quickly ran into the water to swim. When later they looked back at the shore, they noticed that Alex had arrived. He waved to them and was soon swimming also. Ellen thought to herself that he was a handsome and desirable man. When he rejoined them at their blanket afterwards, he said, "I must say that swim was so invigorating."

An hour later Jeff and Nancy indicated they were going to shower and rest before lunch. "See you later, folks."

Now alone, Alex turned to Ellen, "You look lovely today, Ellen. Bikinis were made for you." Ellen blushed.

Ellen placed her straw hat on her head and quietly thanked him. "Cat got your tongue?" he said. "You're probably wondering if it is a simple compliment or a come-on."

Ellen then got a little testy, "You have no idea what I'm thinking, Alex."

"Ellen, please don't do that. I don't want you to be uncomfortable with me."

Her hat tilted on her head as she adjusted it. Moving quickly, she added, "I am confused. Did you come to this place for a specific reason or was it to really get away from all your law books?"

He did not readily answer. When he did, his response was almost sheepish. "I came because of you."

"Alex, you are a married man. Are you trying to seduce me?" She simply had to say what she was thinking.

"Ellen, truthfully, since our first dinner on that rainy night when I saw you with all your rain gear, well..." He stopped and looked at her in a manner she would have called longing. "I can't help what my thoughts of you are."

He tried taking her hand, but she pulled away. "We mustn't do this" she whispered.

"I see where you said 'we'," he smiled.

"I'm not insensitive to attractions, but..."

"Since we are alone now and no one can see us, I'm going to do what I want to do without listening to your feeble excuses." His arms engulfed her and his kiss was such a searing one that she could not help but respond with all her sexual energy. As close as they were to each other now, her heart began beating rapidly. She could not speak.

"Tell me again about unexpected attractions" he said, as his hands moved up and down her arms, while kissing her mouth, her neck, and her shoulders.

Although she felt the same sensation as he, she whispered, "Alex, please."

"That's just what I'm trying to do now. To please you and myself."

She was almost limp in his arms as he continued softly, "I can't help if I'm captivated by you. People are often attracted to more than one person. It's not that unusual. Frankly, I've never done this before. Believe me." He caressed her face. "Beautiful Ellen." Again, he kissed her in such a fashion that she would have allowed him anything. Over and over she whispered "Alex".

When her straw hat fell by her side, she never noticed. They were both so enthralled. Her sensibilities finally prevailed and she said, "Let's go back."

He startled her by saying, "I'm coming to your room tonight, so be ready."

"But, Alex..." He shushed her and then arose. Ellen also arose, picked up her hat, put on her cover-up, and walked slowly ahead of him.

Jeff and Nancy were there and greeted them. Nancy said, "After so much swimming, you must be hungry, Alex?" Briefly looking at Ellen, he smiled, "I have a terrible hunger." With all the chatter, only Ellen grasped his meaning.

Ellen looked down, eating her meal quietly. What could she do after lunch to occupy her time? She did not want the others to see them together again. "Nancy, do you want to go shopping after lunch?" Nancy agreed quickly. Alex looked at Ellen, but said nothing about the shopping suggestion.

Ellen and Nancy spent a long pleasant afternoon gallivanting around town. The two women both had a flair for fashion and could have spent many dollars. Luckily, they knew enough to control themselves. When they returned, they found Alex sitting on the back deck reading a book. Jeff had gone back to the water for more swimming. For Ellen it was truly a delight to see how Nancy and Jeff greeted each other after they were separated even for a short time. Jeff kissed his wife, played with her hair, and said aloud, "Missed you, honey." Ellen let the display flow through her and smiled quietly.

Alex turned to Ellen. "Was it a fruitful afternoon?"

Ellen was in good humor and responded, "We are here to help the local economy. What can I say?" She turned to Nancy, "Am I right, Nancy?" Nancy smiled and nodded.

Alex laughed. "Anybody here want to go to the movies tonight?" he asked.

Jeff said, "We'll pass". With arms entwined, they both left the dining room.

"That leaves just you and me, Ellen" said Alex.

"Well, I certainly don't want to spend time in my room."

He looked at her quizzically and whispered, "There are certain advantages to doing that, you know?"

When she realized what she had said, she turned away from him. Aloud, Alex said, "The movie starts at 7:30 p.m., Ellen."

In the dining room, Ellen tried to strike up a conversation with the Pennsylvania couple who were seated at a far table. They pretty much kept to themselves. "Alex has talked me into going to the movies. Are you interested?" The couple shook their heads. With a sigh, she turned to Alex and said, "I guess it's just you and me. However, I'll pay my own way. Okay with you?"

"Just fine" he replied.

"Do you want to ride to the movie house, Ellen? I'm familiar with this town and the place is way over the other side of town." Ellen agreed.

When they got into his car, he quickly drove away. Ellen was not acquainted with the area, so she said nothing about their destination.

After a bit, she asked how much farther it was. Alex turned and faced her. "I won't lie to you, Ellen. We are not going to the movies. We're going someplace where we can talk freely."

"Alex, are you joking? You said the movies and I thought you were an honorable man. Take me back to the inn."

"Ellen, don't do that. God, I've been thinking of you since we first met."

She was angry now. "Please take me back."

He stopped the car on an isolated place near the pier. "Do you understand what is happening here? I've never been unfaithful to my wife, but you are doing something to me that has never happened before. I told you that when I kissed you earlier today. And I could feel how beautifully you were responding to me. Believe me, I've met women in business and socially, but I've never had this sort of feeling. You... I don't know what to say about you, Ellen."

Her anger subsided some. She placed her head down and said, "Alex, I've never been in a situation like this. Do you understand? If I sleep with you, then what happens after that or when your family returns?"

"Please, Ellen, don't deny me." He looked at her. "Say something."

"Yes, I am attracted to you, but I'm so afraid of the aftermath and the consequences."

He murmured, "It sounds so trite, but can someone fall in love oo quickly?" His hands were on her shoulders. "Do you hear me? I want you."

As he started up the car for their return to the inn, Alex looked at her and simply said, "Leave your bedroom door open tonight. I'll be there soon." He placed his right hand over hers. Ellen said nothing.

When they returned to the inn, she got out of the car and went to her room. Alex went on, seeking a parking place. Although the lights were on a dimmer, there was no one in the main rooms. Once in her room, Ellen did as he suggested and left the door unlocked.

She moved about her room restlessly and with great apprehension. What was she doing? Yes, she was attracted to him.

Then she saw the door knob turn and quickly he was before her. Quietly, he locked the door and turned to her, saying nothing. His mouth and tongue said it all. She responded because she knew how much she wanted this. "Alex, I..." He wouldn't let her finish her sentence. "Just the feel of you is arousing me," he said.

She ardently returned his kisses, as they hurriedly disrobed. Wherever he touched her, the same feeling for him became hers. "How lucky am I having you this way. Your entire body is as beautiful as you are," he said. Then he quickly moved her to her bed. He could no longer wait to consummate his desire for her. Their passion for each other was so intense that it did not take long for her to climax. Thereafter, he too groaned as he gave in to his release.

There was a sudden quiet in the room Finally, he said, "I'd like to sleep here tonight." "Yes, yes" she said breathlessly. Alex smiled, "You've confirmed everything I had thought about you. You're incredible, love. Incredible."

With their arms around each other, they finally fell asleep. In the early morning he awakened and whispered, "Ellen". With her eyes closed, she sleepily answered "Yes?"

He kissed her first on one eyelid, and then the other. Smiling, she opened her eyes as he pulled her to him. "I want to begin my day with you once more, love."

She melted in his arms. Then seductively, she said, "Whatever you say, counselor." Her wanting him now was as great as his wanting her.

Early Monday morning, each left in his own car. Alex admonished Ellen about driving carefully, especially with the onslaught of autos leaving for home after the long weekend. The last thing he told her was, "See you back in town. We'll have dinner then. Okay?"

However, she did not see him for several days, knowing his work load was heavy.

When they reconvened the following Thursday at the hotel dining room, he suggested another brief excursion to the same place the upcoming weekend. "We can leave Friday night and return Sunday night." Then he looked into her eyes. "Shall I get one room or two?" Ellen did not reply, but Alex noticed a slight smile on her face. "Don't be concerned, love, I'll take care of everything."

As expected, their return the following weekend to the same bed and breakfast proved so blissful. There were quiet moments and then incessant talk. They were two people in love and oblivious to everyone. However, early on Sunday morning as they started their walk into town with their arms intertwined, Alex's cell phone rang. When he answered, Ellen knew it was one of his family members. Alex's face looked anguished. He ended his call by saying, I'll get a flight out in the morning." He hung up.

Ellen questioned him. "What's wrong?" He took her hand. "My family is vacationing in the Upper Peninsula of Michigan. My son has been hospitalized with a broken arm. I must go to him."

They returned to their room. While Alex called the airlines, Ellen packed their things. Quickly, their weekend time had shortened and they wasted no time returning to town. Ellen saw how harried he looked. "I'll call you when I can, love." He hurriedly left her outside her hotel lobby. He was worried.

Alone once more in her hotel room, Ellen pondered her dilemma. This was what it was like to be in love with a married man. She tried not to dwell on the difficult circumstances, but she knew it did not bode well. With Alex gone, all her movements were desultory in manner. She sat before her television for hours. Never had she been in such a predicament. In bed, she tossed and turned. Sleep was long in coming.

Upon awakening in the morning, she was still greatly troubled. However. It was Monday and she still had many company facilities to visit. She went on with her work routine Monday, Tuesday and Wednesday. Without word from Alex, she was getting more anxious every day. Finally, from Michigan on Wednesday night, he called her at her hotel.

He explained that his son's arm was broken, but it had been a clean break and complete recovery was assured. Ellen commiserated with him. He said he had to catch up on his work upon return and probably would not be able to see her until the weekend. Ellen said she understood. Then they hung up.

At one of the satellite offices she met up with an old friend, Don. They were able to catch up on old times. He suggested dinner Thursday night at a Thai restaurant he knew well. Ellen agreed to his invitation.

Don was a fun guy who made having dinner with him a pleasure. Don could not console her, but he enabled her to relax and for them to have a few laughs together. Much of their conversation was about company matters. When he took her back to her hotel, Ellen explained how she had enjoyed her evening with him. Shortly thereafter, Don left.

When Ellen entered her hotel, someone at the front desk called her. There was a message for her. "I was worried about you, love. Did you go out to dinner? Call when you can." Obviously, he had returned earlier than planned.

She was subdued when she returned Alex's call. "Ellen, I'm sorry about what happened. I had to see for myself. He's doing all right and will be able to continue with his vacation. Hope you understand, love." However, upon hearing her. quiet response, he said: "I had to see him. He's my son."

"Alex, I do understand." Before she could say more, he said: "Dinner then tomorrow night?" Ellen replied: "I have a long day, but I will be back here at about 6 p.m. See you then."

* * *

143

When she returned on Friday evening after a long day, Alex was sitting in the lobby. Ellen was pleasantly surprised to see him. She moved rapidly to where he was sitting. "Can I come up to your room, love?"

She smiled and took his hand. Seeing him made her heart do somersaults and she truly was happy to see him.

Once in her room, she asked: "Can we sit and talk a bit?"

"Of course." Then he said: "Did my situation throw you off course?"

"Frankly, yes. I was flying high with you and then reality shot me down."

Alex rose from his chair and went to her, hugging her tightly. "God, I love you much, Ellen. I don't know what to say. You've known about my family from the beginning. I can never abandon them."

"That's true, but I never saw beyond us. I forgot that there are additional people you love. I'm sorry. Truly." She laid her closed eyes against his chest.

Alex kissed her on the forehead. "Don't apology, love. It is what it is." He cupped her face so he could look into her eyes. "What do you want to do?"

"I don't know," she whispered. "I just don't know." Her arms went around his neck and his kiss seared through her.

When she then stepped back, she said, "I have to take a shower after this long day."

"Do you want to go out to dinner afterwards?" he asked.

As she went off to shower, she replied, "Whatever, you say."

After showering, she wrapped the towel around her body and came back into the room. Alex's clothes were on the nearby chair. Then she turned.

Ellen was surprised to see Alex already in bed. She smiled ruefully: "You certainly are sly."

"I know. But if you don't come to me immediately, you will pay later," he smiled back.

Ellen sauntered around the room. "I'll think about it," she joked.

Alex quickly arose from the bed and pulled the towel away from her body. He stood looking at her for a moment. "Now that's what I want to see." His voice softened as he pulled her to him. "Much, much better, I'd say. I want every bit of you."

Ellen put her arms around his waist and slowly moved them all the way down his back. Then she squeezed him towards her.

Alex laughed as she did that. "The lady knows what she wants." In turn, he did the very same to her.

Without another word, he picked her up in his arms. With one arm under her torso and the other under her legs, they returned to bed. Ellen's arms went around his neck and she whispered in his ear "yes." He loved touching her, as he did now. She could not do otherwise as her hands moved over this sensual man.

"My desire for you is maddening," he growled as he pulled her closer still. They never went to dinner, but their evening together was exquisite.

She had never felt so wanted as when he made love to her. As for Alex, he was quite sated and happy. Being in love for them had been an extraordinary experience, but now there was reality to deal with. Time was running out for them. As always, he held her close to him. " I love you much, Ellen. I love you much."

* * *

As often as possible, they would meet for dinner or rendezvous in Ellen's hotel room, where he sometimes would stay overnight. While thinking of all that had occurred in these months, she realized her time here was rapidly coming to an end. This had been an extraordinary experience for her. She had found Alex. Now she had to remember it was all ending. This had not been a summer romance. She was enough of a realist to know they must now part for good. No happy-ever-after for them. They were going in different directions. She tortured herself thinking of never seeing him again. Her heart ached and her mind could not see its way out of this morass. It had been so brief, but stunningly beautiful. Sadly, it would soon be over.

When she next met Alex, he suggested they go somewhere quiet and without people about. Neither was hungry. He held her hand tightly.

"What about we walk by the water?" he suggested. She looked so forlorn and could barely talk. Tears glistened on her eyelids. All sorts of boats were bobbing in the water and plying their good fortune, while her fortune was sinking.

For some unknown reason, she had brought her straw hat with her. Their sadness was palpable. What more could they say as they continued walking. Without thinking, she stopped and threw her straw hat into the water. Alex looked at what she had done. Turning to him, she said, "Let it go wherever it wants to go. I can't change its direction now nor certain events."

He placed his arms around her shoulder. All he could say was, "Oh, my love." He knew what her thoughts were. Now he had to say something to allay her anguish and his. Unfortunately, it had to be said now. There was no more time left for them.

"You know you have changed the trajectory of my life" he said. "Now, I have to get back on track for many reasons." Sadly, he looked at her. "You know that, love, don't you?" He waited for her reply. She did not. He continued, "My family is returning in a couple of days from their vacation. You will be leaving soon with your work here finished and be back on home territory."

She moved in his arms and opened her mouth to say something. Instead, he stopped her with a kiss. "I'll miss you terribly, but you will always be in a part of my heart. I had no idea meeting you would be so beautiful, especially what has happened between us. I love you much, Ellen. I love you much.

"If we had met a long time ago, I would never have let you go. Now I have people in my life whom I also love and I must be back with them. My wife is a great woman. My children are the best part of my life and a joy beyond explanation. They are the reason I work so hard. I want their future to be the very best possible."

Again, his eyes were focused on her. "I don't mean this to be a soliloquy, but I can't stop saying I love you much. This has been an extraordinary time for me and it's all because of you, love." His lips were on her forehead.

With teary eyes Ellen said, "I'll always love you much, Alex."

"No, Ellen, no. Robert has wanted to marry you for some time. You said he is a great guy and you are very fond of him. Make a life with him. I don't want you to be alone. I want you to be happy. As happy as possible."

Then he sighed, "You have brought a beautiful dimension to my life and it makes this decision very painful for me. Each time I said 'I love you much' I meant it most sincerely. Do you understand, love?" They were holding hands tightly and couldn't seem to let go.

Ellen was bereft. Suddenly, with the finality of his words, she turned away from him and steeled herself not to look back. She had to find a place alone where she could unleash the tears and bear the heartbreak simultaneously.

"Alex, please leave now". Reluctantly, he did as she suggested. He walked away. Usually, he would turn and blow her a kiss. This time he did not. He simply moved farther and farther away from her. She was left alone.

* * *

When Ellen walked off the plane, there was Robert. Wonderfully reliable Robert. Always waiting for her to return home from a business trip. He rushed to her, took her carry-on, hugged her tightly and kissed her on the cheek. "Boy, am I glad to see you. I missed you terribly." Ellen smiled. He always said that.

"Have you thought over my marriage proposal?" he said hurriedly.

"Yes, yes, very often. After I get home, rest a bit, report to the office, and get things in order, I will give you my answer". Then again, she smiled at him. She had to pull herself together.

Turning to her, Robert continued, "You look tired, Ellen."

Softly, she replied, "Yes, it was rather exhausting, but a truly pleasant experience." Again, she looked at him and smiled.

"You don't know how I counted the days waiting for you to return to me," he whispered. Ellen placed her head on his shoulder and there was another hug from him.

"Actually, I enjoyed every aspect of my time there," she continued. "The people I engaged with were all very nice to me. However, as unforgettable as it was, now I have to move on. I can't look back."

As they walked away, arm in arm, her smile indicated to him that he would be getting a positive response to his marriage proposal.

Ellen was thinking that just a few hours ago, she had been heartbroken. She now had to color her responses so that what had transpired was all simply in the past tense. All that had happened had to be placed away in the back of her mind. Robert would become her future. She had always loved Robert, perhaps not with the passion she had loved Alex. She would probably never see Alex again, but what occurred between them was extraordinarily sweet and beautiful although short-lived. It was an interlude she would never know again. Although her thoughts would surely bring her back to Alex now and then, what would define her from now on was what lay ahead. Life with Robert.

EPILOGUE

Four-year-old Charlotte was running around the house trying to catch her little dog. "Mommy. Mommy, I can't catch him. Please catch him for me."

"Catch what, Charlotte?" said her mother.

"My dog, Brandi."

"Honey, he can't run out of the house. He'll come to you soon."

Ellen was doing her chores and glancing now and again at the television she had turned on earlier. There were some congressional people spouting their usual rhetoric. She recognized some of the well-known representatives and senators. Behind them were others. Then she saw him. Alex. His hair was grayer now, but he still was as handsome as ever.

Her heart skipped a beat. So much time had passed. She stared at his image on the screen; she couldn't tear herself away. Many memories. All she could remember him saying was, "Love you much." As the tears trickled down her face, she realized she must not torment herself this way. She turned off the television as Charlotte gleefully ran to her, "I found him, mommy. I found him."

Her mother turned to her and quietly replied, "So did I. So did I."

Call Me By Name

CALL ME BY NAME

any called her Red. She had natural red hair, but she hated that appellation. However, if she made a fuss, they did it all the more. If she said nothing, she would swallow her anger.

Her name was actually Kristen. She had recently graduated from college with a degree in communications. She was a pretty good writer. Seeking a job in that field was a bit of a challenge. Everyone seemed to have chosen that field. However, she was persistent with her resume. She would have gone anywhere for the proper job. They seemed hard to come by.

One day she received a call from the Daily Standard, a local newspaper, where she had sent one of her resumes. They had a job she might want to apply for. It was as an assistant to the advertising editor.

Well, she thought, a foot in the door could be of some help. When she arrived for her interview, she was on her best behavior. All the features of the job were explained to her. She would take ads for people coming into the office or via telephone. She would explain the sizes, prices and duration of the ads. That was pretty much it. Any additional help the advertising editor needed, she would provide.

Kristen decided to say yes to the job. Who knew what the future would hold here for her.

A week later she signed in as an employee of the Daily Standard. Mr. Knowles, the advertising editor, was very accommodating in helping her to adapt insofar as dealing with people who came in person with their needs for an ad. Also, there were the telephone inquiries to handle. In order to put her at ease, he told her "Some people here say, 'Knowles knows best'." Kristen laughed.

She easily took to the job. Some people did telephone their ads, while others came in person with theirs. There were full-page ads. Some were shorter. Others, brief but pithy. Every day she met someone new. Some called her by name and some, of course, called her Red.

She continued to live at home. When she felt comfortable in her work and the prospects seemed good, she decided to get an apartment. Since most rentals were costly, she sought a roommate. Her newspaper's ads provided a plethora of people who, like her, were also seeking a roommate.

After several interviews, she chose a girl named Alicia. She had originally lived in California and was a graphic artist. Alicia had a sweet demeanor about her. She seemed to be easy-going. For their first meeting, they lunched together. Each enumerated her needs and how living arrangements should be for them to co-exist.

They found a two-bedroom furnished apartment with a small kitchen, bath, and cozy living room. They also agreed on the price.

Alicia indicated she was a rather good cook. Perhaps she could do some cooking. It would cut the cost of dining out or ordering take-out. Kristen agreed that it all sounded good to her. All things being equal, Kristen could handle other things. Well, they were in agreement about that. No boredom here. She made some friends at the newspaper office. Socially, some of them, including Alicia, would go off to rock concerts, jazz festivals, little bars for some drinking, dancing, and a few laughs. Some weekends it would be visiting in and around the local environs. Life was falling into place.

Some of the people who periodically came into the office had ads placed in the newspaper. They got to know Kristen better.

Mr. Johnson had a small hardware store that vied with the giants for business. Each Saturday he ran a full-page ad. He indicated his business was going rather well because of the ads. Kristen was pleased to hear that. It meant return business.

Mrs. Rizzoli had an Italian restaurant with a seating capacity of about 100 people. She did well with her ads because word of mouth was that the food at her establishment was good and plentiful. People invariably would bring home leftovers.

One day an attractive young man came to the office. He was dressed entirely in leather. Kristen looked him over. Interesting. Not many younger people came in with ads. She maintained her composure, as she sought to help him.

"Hey, Red, I'd like to place an ad with your newspaper." He smiled at her. A charming smile. He said his name was Mark. He owned a motorcycle shop aptly named Mark's Motorcycles.

"Please give me some details as to what you want, how large an ad you need, what day you want it to run, and for what length of time. Also..."

"Boy" he interrupted "you sure go on and on with your spiel."

"I'm trying to be helpful."

Then he changed his demeanor. "Have you ever been on a motorcycle?"

"No, I have not, but..."

Another interruption. "I can just see that beautiful red hair of yours flying all over the place riding with me."

Kristen laughed. He continued, "Not only is she a beautiful redhead, but she has a delightful laugh too."

"Please, sir, what can I do for you?"

Slyly he said, "Oh, lady, you could do a lot of things for me."

When Kristen blushed, he said, "She even blushes."

She was not making any headway with this man about his ad. "Would you like Mr. Knowles, our advertising editor, to help you, sir?"

"No, no, no. I didn't mean to be flippant, but I never thought I'd meet such a lovely gal like you here." Then he stopped and turned serious. "I prepared my own ad for your newspaper. Look it over." Kristen did. "Is it O.K.?"

"Yes, fine," she told him. "Do you want to pay now or should we bill you?"

He took out his checkbook. While he was writing his check, without looking up, he said, "Have you worked here long?"

"Not very" she replied.

"What is your name?" he asked as he handed her the check. "Kristen" she answered.

"Hi, Kristen. I believe I told you I'm Mark. Please call me that instead of sir since I'll be coming back another day." Shyly, she said, "Thank you...Mark."

As he walked out the door, he turned and smiled, "See you around, Red."

Well, thought Kristen, that was not the kind of individuals she encountered often, but he certainly was brash. Actually, he was a breath of fresh air.

* * *

Her work became routine, but it was pleasant to go to the office each day. Meeting the public was fun and she enjoyed virtually all whom she encountered.

At the end of another week Mark came in again. "Hi, Red, how are you doing?" With a half-smile on her face, she simply said, "Fine."

Listen, I want to run my ad again this weekend. What do you think?"

"Certainly, we can do that. But you know we can set up an account for you so you won't have to come in all the time."

He was amused. "You must be joking. I come in often as I want to see this lovely redhead and you expect me to set up an account. Oh, come on, Red, give a guy a chance."

Kristen blushed. "Now, Mark, I..." In a flirtatious way, Mark said "Keep talking. You intrigue me."

She digressed. "Will you be paying by check?"

As he began to write his check, he looked at her and softly said, "Can I have your home phone number, Red?" "Listen, my name is Kristen," she repeated again.

"I know that, but when I call you Red you get all riled up and I like to see all that emotion." He held out his hand to her. "By the way, here's my check."

Just then the phone rang. Kristen answered. It was someone wanting to place an ad. She waved Mark off.

Reluctantly, Mark left.

Actually, Kristen felt badly talking to him that way. She really should be more pleasant. Yes, she wanted him to place return ads, but he really made her day and allowed her to smile each time he came into the office.

She perused the newspaper every day, checking the many ads the office received. Also, she wanted to check them all to be sure everything was as the clients wanted them.

Kristen looked over Mark's ad for his motorcycle shop. She wondered how good a business he did. Also, what an ebullient man he was. The thought occurred to her that he could be an interesting man to date.

Some days were busier than others. Mr. Knowles was a great boss. All in all, she was happy with her work. Even living with Alicia went well. In fact, they were compatible, so that each week proved a good one.

Sure enough, sometime thereafter Mark again showed up at the office.

"Hey, Red, you're looking more beautiful since I saw you last."

"Oh, stop that."

"You neglected to give me your phone number when I asked you last time."

"Why should I do that?"

"Because I want to take you to lunch today. How about it?"

"I don't know."

"Oh, come on, Red, I'm harmless. It's only lunch."

She looked at him hesitatingly, "O.K. As long as you stop calling me Red."

Mark smiled. "See you outside at 1 p.m. There are places nearby. How about Mexican?" Kristen tilted her head, "Sounds good to me."

He was walking back and forth when she joined him. He took her elbow and found the restaurant readily. They ate with gusto and talked away the time so they could know each other better. "Tell me about yourself, Kristen?"

She proceeded to tell him about her family, her roommate, and her college experience. "This is my first full-time job. How about you?"

"Originally, I came from up north, where my family still lives. Then I went to college. I used to come here to visit my grandparents. This area appealed to me. When I decided on a business, I thought I could make a go of it here. I've always had motorcycles. This seemed the logical spot to start my business."

"Isn't it somewhat dangerous?" she asked.

"Whatever you do, you have to be careful." Then he murmured "Even when you get interested in redheads." Kirsten did not reply. He looked at his watch. "Let's get you back to work." He squeezed her hand. They then exchanged phone numbers. As he walked away, he said, "See you again, sugar."

Two days later at work there was another call. "Hi, Kristen. It's Mark. Thanks for your number. Listen, Saturday night there is a businessmen's dinner-dance. I'd like to take you. If you call me when you get home, I'll give you all the details. Call me ASAP."

When Kristen returned home, she listened to the several calls she had received. Hearing Mark's voice made her perk up. She quickly called him back.

"Kristen, thanks for calling. How was your day?"

"Just fine, Mark. I'm returning your call."

"You heard what I said about Saturday night. Are you available?" When she said yes, he smiled.

"Great. O.K. Here are the details. It's a dress-up affair. Just wear a pretty dress. I'll be in a suit. It starts at 7 p.m., with cocktails followed by dinner. Later there is dancing. Do you have any questions?"

"Are we traveling by motorcycle?"

"No, no" he laughed. "I'll have my car. I'll pick you up at 6:30. Any other questions?" She said no. He concluded the call. "See you Saturday."

Sure enough, promptly at 6:30 Saturday night, he was at her apartment. When Mark saw Kristen, a big grin appeared on his face. She wore a green sheath with a little jacket. "You look lovely" he said.

In his car, he said, "What I should have said is that you look absolutely gorgeous." He started up the car. "Let's get the show on the road."

They were going to a local hotel for the dinner-dance. He knew several of the business men and he introduced Kristen. With her beautiful red hair, she stood out among the other women.

When they found their table, they chatted with all the other people who surrounded them and whom Mark knew. Kristen thought it was all so pleasant. Conversation went at a good pace. Even the meal was excellent.

The orchestra began playing for the dancing patrons. Kristen took off her little jacket. The green sheath was strapless. Against her white skin and red hair, Mark could not believe his eyes. She commanded most everyone's attention.

Arising from his seat and taking her hand, he said, "I believe this dance is mine, mademoiselle." With his arm around her waist, jokingly he continued, "I didn't think a guy like me would get this much attention from all these people." Kristen laughed.

"God certainly knew what he was doing when he created you" Mark whispered in her ear. "You are a beautiful woman, dear Kristen."

He held her tight and whirled her around the dance floor. "Hope none of these guys wants to cut in. I'll have to annihilate them." Again, Kristen was amused.

The evening was totally enjoyable. Kristen was happy at the turn of events. Mark was over the moon. After much camaraderie and laughter, Kristen and Mark left around midnight.

En route to her apartment, he told her he did not want the evening to end so soon. She squeezed his hand.

"Let's go someplace for a few drinks" he said.

"Whatever you say, Mark."

"There's a lot more I want to know about you, but we'll do this slowly, Kristen."

At the next establishment there were more drinks, bantering, and sweet kisses between them.

"Want to go motorcycling with me sometime soon?"

Kristen hesitated. "Would it be safe for me? I've never been on one."

"Absolutely safe. How about next Sunday?"

So the date was set for their next encounter. He took her to her door and kissed her once more. "Thanks for tonight, Kristen."

"Oh, no, thanks for inviting me. Mark, I really enjoyed myself."

In bed that night as she went over the entire evening, she smiled and fell asleep.

His motorcycle was revving up. He was waiting for his passenger. When he heard the apartment door open, he looked up. Kristen was coming down the stairs to join him. As he had told her on the phone, he asked that she wear jeans and a sweater.

He liked to greet her with a happy face. "Hi, Red, how are you doing today?" She smiled. He continued, "Ready to go?" She nodded.

"Wait," he said. "Need to put on these helmets before we ride, one for you; one for me." He helped her adjust the helmet he had brought for her. Also, he made the seat behind him comfortable for her.

"I've never been on a motorcycle," she said apprehensively.

"It will be the ride of your life. You'll be quite safe. Hang on tightly to my waist." She did as she was told.

When they drove away, she began to feel the breeze whirling all around her, She was apprehensive, but held tightly to Mark. That gave her a secure feeling.

They rode for some time. He chose byways where most automobiles did not traverse. She relaxed somewhat. Although the countryside seemed to fly by, she began to like the feel of it. She was not constrained by the confines of an automobile. It was all quite enjoyable. Not at all as she imagined it would be.

After they had ridden for a couple of hours, Mark slowed down and stopped by the side of a road.

"want some lunch?"

"Yes, but let it be my treat," she replied.

"Of course not. Let's see, there is a hamburger joint at the next corner. We'll stop there."

As he maneuvered his cycle to the small restaurant, he said, "Will a hamburger and a drink do?"

"Yes."

When they seated themselves, he asked her what she thought of the ride.

"It was exhilarating. Thanks for showing me how exciting that sort of ride can be."

"You're welcome."

They talked about a variety of things. "Ready for a little more of the same?" he said.

"Yes," she said eagerly.

She had no idea where they were off to this time, but she placed herself in his care.

When they finally came to a small secluded knoll by the sea, they stopped and sat side by side on the grass.

"Isn't Mother Nature beautiful?" he sighed.

"I agree."

When he placed both his arms around her and drew her to him, he whispered "Mother Nature certainly did a beautiful job with you." He kissed her sweetly. She responded. His kisses became more eager and wanting.

He placed her down on the grass. His hands went under her clothing. "You are doing things to me, Kristen. I want you now."

Her heart was beating rapidly. "Mark, I need to tell you something."

He looked at her for a moment, waiting to hear what she had to say.

"Mark, I've never slept with a man."

He did not know what to say. "This is a predicament, Kristen."

"Don't be angry, she implored.

"Why should I be angry? However, this is not the place for us to make love, at least not for you." He ran his hands through his hair. "Kristen, let's go to my apartment. And please don't be afraid."

He pulled her up from the grass. He kissed her passionately, let her go, and then moved to his motorcycle nearby.

"There's more to come, sweet Kristen."

As they motored back to town, she found herself holding tightly to him. She did not know what to think.

When they arrived at his apartment, they dismounted from the cycle. He held her hand and kissed both hands as if to reassure her.

In his bedroom he could sense her awkwardness. "Kristen, this is the most natural thing in the world between men and women. When you want me to stop, I will. However, at this point I am beyond wanting to stop"

She knew they were past that particular barrier. She wanted him. This great desire for him filled her body. Their kisses were a give and take sort of thing. She gave; he tool. He gave; she took. Their arms were intertwined. She kept murmuring his name. When he could wait no longer, he entered her. She did not cry out. She simply moaned in pleasure. He allowed it all to linger. She wanted more. And more is what she got. He couldn't have been happier.

Much later, as they continued to lie in bed he looked out the window., "Kristen, it's getting dark. Why don't you stay here for the night. "I'll bring you back to the office in the morning. Please say yes."

"No, Mark, I think…"

"Oh, keep quiet. I don't like the word 'no'."

She was still glowing from all that had transpired between them. "I have to be there at 9 a.m."

"Baby, my motorcycle will fly to get you to your job. O.K.?" He hugged her tightly. "Now, I have another suggestion. It's almost supper time and…"

"I can whip up something if you show me what's in your fridge."

As he pulled on his briefs, he said, "Here's my bathrobe. Put it on. Then we can take it from there."

She said nothing. She went to the fridge. He had eggs, some leftover vegetables. Grated cheese, and a few other things. "I can make us an omelet."

"The kitchen is all yours. Your kisses, however, are mine." He kissed her on the nose.

Knowing her way around kitchens, she proceeded to prepare the omelet with some of the leftover vegetables. When done, she placed it in a large platter. With the lettuce, she simply place it in a bowl. She found the dressing for it. Everything was placed on the table, while Mark scurried to get dishes, utensils, glasses and napkins. "How am I doing, Red?"

"Call me by name."

"O.K. Beautiful." He stopped. "How about beer?"

For a hurried meal, it turned out quite well.

"Now, for dessert, you have a choice. I have ice cream or you take all of me."

She laughed. "I'm thinking, I'm thinking."

"Isn't that an old vaudeville routine?"

Kristen stood up to clear the dishes, etc. while he placed them all in the dishwasher. Then he ran it. "Come on,. Let's sit and watch some television."

They sat side by side on his couch. While the news droned on, she saw him begin to doze. She did not stir from his side. She sat and thought of all the day's events. From motorcycling, to making love for the first time, to this evening meal. Now she was just sitting here and letting it all flow into her. Mark had truly made this such a very special day for her. She hoped all that had transpired this day would continue for them.

When he finally awakened, he said, "Sorry about that." They continued to watch television for more than an hour after that. "Do you want to go to bed? It's been quite a long and great day." She nodded.

He always liked to joke. "As I said earlier about dessert... Did you decide?

"I'll take all of you."

"Splendid choice. You have very good taste. Remember, I'm dangerous."

Later in bed she found he was not dangerous. He allowed her to learn and enjoy the intimacy between them. She thought he was incredible, and she turned to him and told him so.

The next morning, as promised, he took her to work. As she floated into the office, Mr. Knowles said, "You must have had a wonderful day yesterday?"

"Mr. Knowles, you'll never know."

165

What Mr. Knowles did not know was that Kristen and Mark began to date regularly. They would go out to dinner, the movies, concerts and the like. Both were eager to see each other often. If he was not busy at work, he would call her and exchange the day's news and other pleasantries. If she had things to do, she would call him and tell him what she was going to do, so he would not worry when he could not contact her. Life at this stage was glorious for them.

He was a great swimmer and he insisted Kristen come out to see him swim at the pool. She saw how well he navigated the waters. Also, he liked softball. She would cheer him on as he played shortstop for a local city team. They might go on picnics together. Other times they even visited museums. Or they just would spend an evening watching television. As to personality, he was more outgoing than she was. She certainly was not the risk taker he was. Although, overall, their interests were pretty much the same.

The days turned into months. The months became more months. And so went their romance. They were very much in love. Sometimes he would bring her small bouquets of flowers. Like a typical woman, she got sentimental when he did that. When she stroked his cheek with her hand, he quickly captured it and kissed it.

As life would have it, there were also days when things did not turn out so well. In some instances, they had differences of opinions. When he would pull her into his arms after these skirmishes, lovemaking always won out.

One particular day, Kristen turned up at Mark's apartment. She was all out of sorts. It had been a bad day at work.

When he opened his door, he greeted her in a happy way. "Hi, beautiful. How are you?" He hugged her.

She was grumpy. "Fine."

"Oh, come on, sugar, things aren't that bad."

"Stop that" she shouted. "You address me as sweetie, honey, baby...and other names. Call me by name."

He stepped back. "O.K. Whatever you say."

When he stood away from her, his voice softened. "How about my addressing you as 'wife'?"

"What?"

"You heard me."

She stepped back, startled. He was proposing to her and she had reacted so badly. Her hands went to her face and she began crying.

"Mark, I'm so sorry. I shouldn't be taking out my frustrations on you." She hesitated. A smile lit up her face. "Please, say it all again."

"You always say 'call me by name' so I thought calling you 'wife' would be the best way to address you. What do you think?"

She ran to his arms. "I love you, Mark. Yes, yes, yes. 'Wife' sounds absolutely wonderful."

"Kristen, you know how I feel about you. Together we could make a great team." Then he caressed her. "You're the best thing that's ever happened to me. I've never wanted a woman like I want you. I love you very much, dear Kristen. Is forever with you too much to hope for?"

"Oh, Mark, I love you too. I won't be grumpy again, I promise." They hugged each other tightly.

"Who are you fooling? I know you well, Red. Sorry... Kristen."

Then he touched her face and added "I never thought I'd prefer a redhead. Redheads get a lot of attention. Some even have a temper. What am I going to do about that?"

"Live with it or stop seeing me" she said smugly. Then she laughed. The turn of events elated her.

"Listen, sweetie, do you think I'm crazy. I happen to love this redhead." Then he reached for her. "She also tastes very good" he smiled as his lips hungrily sought hers again and again. Kristen responded with all her heart.

* * *

They were married in a simple ceremony with a small coterie of family and friends under an arbor by the sea. She walked down a small aisle to where he stood waiting for her. A simple white gown and a wreath of flowers on her head was her wedding outfit. He was wearing a light suit and smiling broadly. He took her hand tightly in his. They made their vows.

"I, Kristen, take thee, Mark, etc. etc." Then the judge stated aloud that they were man and wife.

After a small reception, they flew to the Caribbean for their long-awaited honeymoon—their glorious, loving honeymoon. This was the beginning of their life together.

Back home his apartment became their home. They made a number of changes, painting, buying new furniture, and some renovations. They were the typical newlyweds, enjoying this new phase of their lives.

In bed at night Mark was surprised at how Kristen had become a sensuous woman. He would often tease her by saying, "My little virgin knows what she likes and I like all of that too."

Sometimes there were heated differences, but as he often said, "Love conquers all." Money was something they had to be careful about despite Mark's having his own cycle business. They wanted many material things, but they wanted them yesterday. Another day might bring them what they wanted.

After a while they seemed to be doing fairly well, but Kristen always worried about their finances. One night, Mark came home full of enthusiasm. "Listen, honey, Chester's Cycle is up for sale. It's about forty miles from here. It's in a beach resort area and we probably could make a go of it. What do you think?"

Kristen glared at him. "I don't think so. We haven't yet pulled ourselves completely out of this money hole and you have the gall to think about another business. Negative. Negative."

He glared back at her. "You could be a bit more enthusiastic about the entire idea."

Her retort was, "You may not like the word 'no', but I say 'no'."

"Look, there's no harm in looking into it." He was raising his voice.

"Don't be so flippant about everything," she replied. "You make everything seem so easy."

"You have to take chances in life. If you saw it my way you might think it's a great opportunity. I'm going there tomorrow to get more details."

"Well, I'm not coming" she said angrily.

The rest of the day was a testy one. At mealtime, they barely spoke. She banged cupboard doors. He went out and slammed the front door. When he returned late, she was in bed, already asleep. He often kissed her good night, but right now he was seething. Reasoning with her was difficult.

The next day he motored to Chester's Cycles to check the feasibility of buying the business. The owner was retiring and was anxious to sell. Mark thought because of this, bargaining about the price put him at an advantage. Other details seemed propitious. After talking with the owner, walking through the place, and having all of his questions answered, he returned home.

He greeted Kristen, but said nothing more about what had ensued. At dinner all he said was "Sounds good." He wanted her feedback.

This time Kristen was furious. He was shocked. She had never done that before. He answered her quickly, "Are you having hormonal problems? Or is this a bigger problem for you than you will admit?"

She stopped eating, arose from her chair, and went into the living room. He followed her, "Honey, this is not like you. We've always been able to talk over everything." He was doing his best to placate her.

"I don't want to hear anything more from you" she replied.

Another bad day, he thought. He didn't know how to reason with her. He left the room.

Later, when Mark stirred and turned around in bed, he gently placed his arm on his wife's side of the bed. There was no one there. He sat up. Where was she? He rubbed his eyes and got up, looking for her. According to the bedside clock, it was after 2 a.m.

He went into the living room. She was huddled on the sofa in her bath robe, almost in a fetal position. He shook her gently. "Honey, what are you doing here? Come to bed."

"No" she said emphatically.

"What do you mean 'no'?"

"I'm so angry at you about that new business idea of yours. You know we can't really afford to open another cycle shop."

"Look, it's late. We both have to get up early" he said. He proceeded to get her up. She would not move.

"Kristen, come to bed. I promise we'll talk about it in the morning."

He had tried talking calmly to her, but without effect. He began to pick her up.

She argued, "I said 'no'."

"Look, you know you should be in our bed. Certainly, not out here on an uncomfortable couch."

She struggled, as he brought her into the bedroom and to their bed. "Now, take off that robe and try to sleep properly." She continued to resist. He finally was able to take her bathrobe off. When he did and looked at her nakedness, he began to kiss her. "My dear, you'll never get away from me. You know what you are doing to me right now."

"I said no." She tried to ward him off.

"You know I don't like the word 'no'."

The more he touched her in all the right places, the more she knew she would not be able to resist him.

"If I call you 'Red' or 'baby' or 'sweetie' will you get really angry and aroused?" he teased her.

She said, "You know I never can win with you. When you are this close, my resistance is low."

"That's what I love about you. Your resistance may be low, but I enjoy you when you are nice and hot, like right now."

When he touched her body again and again, she knew this was where she wanted to be. She loved the feel of him and ran her hands all over him. Soon they were joined. Making love with great intensity always gave them the utmost pleasure.

After a time, they separated. He saw tears in her eyes. She clung to him. "Maybe sometimes I look at matters in a gloomy fashion, but don't ever leave me" she insisted. "I love you, Mark. I love you."

"Kristen, I will never leave you. Never!"

Mark mulled over this dilemma. He wanted to take a chance. The business seemed promising. His wife, however, was adamantly against it. She was afraid they would be inundated with debt and not be able to handle it. He did not know how to mollify her, yet still go ahead with this opportunity.

One day he had a light bulb moment. To keep Kristin happy there could be a compromise. Maybe a lease for a year or two could be advantageous for all. He would see if he could make a go of it. He did not want to deal with an unhappy wife. He needed Kristen on his side wholeheartedly. He would talk to the owner of Chester's Cycles.

He hurried home. Kristen was already there. He burst into the kitchen, grinning. Then he picked her up and twirled her around and around.

"Put me down" she shouted. "Lovemaking does not solve our problem."

"I believe I have a solution we can both live with." Before she could reply, he said, "Hear me out."

He enumerated his idea of a lease arrangement to her. "How does that sound?"

For the first time in days, he saw a very small smile cross her face.

"Honey, I love you. I want you to be happy."

Slowly she said, "I have a very persuasive husband." He put her down. She approached him and folded her arms around his neck. "Since I get a discount for advertising in our newspaper, I'm going to place a large one saying that I love my husband."

"Don't be funny. Just be on my side" he insisted. Finally, he said, "Let's go for a motorcycle ride."

The country side was so forgiving as they rode for miles and miles. All the cobwebs were being tossed out of their lives.

* * *

When the police called her one night, she could not believe what she heard. Mark had been in an accident. She rushed to the scene. His motorcycle had hit an embankment. He had not seen it when he swerved to avoid an oncoming vehicle. His motorcycle had hit the embankment hard. The EMS were already there. Mark was on a stretcher. She heard him moaning. She bent down to be close to him.

"I hurt so much. There's pain everywhere." Whatever he said was labored. "So much pain. Help me."

172

She did not know what to say. She held his hand tightly. Then she bent down to kiss him. She thought he might recognize her if she said, "Mark, call me by name."

In all his pain, he knew who she was. "Kristen. Kristen."

Then he gave a great sigh. His head turned to one side.

The EMS personnel looked at each other and then looked down at him.

Mark had lost consciousness.

When the EMS people realized that he was in grave condition, they gently pulled Kristen back. They needed to put Mark's body on a gurney and rush him to a hospital. Kristen tried to fling herself forward so that she could touch Mark. The EMS people held her as she screamed "Mark, call me sugar, Red or sweetie." She was gulping and sobbing loudly. Again, she cried out, "Mark, please call me anything."

For several weeks Mark was hospitalized and in rehab. Kristen visited him every day. Though he was not conscious for several days, he finally awakened, one day, calling out her name. She was not there when that happened. Since his accident she promised herself that she would keep his business open. She made some inquiries and found a man who knew the motorcycle business. His name was Louis. Arrangements were finally made for him to take over while Mark recovered. Kristen was kept quite busy between her job at the newspaper and going to Mark's motorcycle shop to help Louis with paper work and anything he needed. Luckily, Louis knew the business well.

She had not known much about Mark's business but she made a great effort to learn. Between visits to the hospital, her job, tending to things at home, and matters at the motorcycle shop, she often found herself exhausted at the end of the day. She had to keep going for her husband, Mark. The mere thought of his being incapacitated and unable to work again haunted her. It must not happen. She had to prove to him that she could be his helpmate.

Another day he awakened and saw her sitting by his bedside. He smiled broadly. "Kristen, my Kristen." He was getting weepy, but she would not allow him to do that.

"Everything is going to be all right, Mark. I have someone working at your shop, waiting for your return."

He was concerned, "Does he know what he is doing?"

"Yes" she reassured him. "He knows motorcycles well. He is retired and actually enjoying that work again." She caressed his face. "Besides, he has a great helper in me."

"You! You're working in my shop? Wow! What great news." He sat up to take her face in his hands. "My beautiful Kristen."

"I'll do whatever you say, boss." She repeated, "What do you think, boss?"

Mark looked at her, "No you don't. I expect you to call me by name."

Some Wednesday Night

SOME WEDNESDAY NIGHT

e looked across the room at the many people that were at the affair. It was a large dance party and most people were, of course, dancing. From the sidelines he looked to the left, to the right, and straight ahead. People certainly enjoyed the rhythms emanating from the orchestra. It was a nice night, perfect for an event of this kind.

When there was a break in the crowd, he saw her. She was dancing with an acquaintance of his. He smiled. She was beautiful. He made some long strides to where they were.

"Hey, Nick," he said, "can I cut in?"

"Sure" said Nick.

The music was starting anew and he said, "Shall we?"

She smiled sweetly, "Of course."

He held her close and began asking her many questions.

"What's your name?"

"Angel" she replied.

"An appropriate name for a lovely woman like you."

Again, she smiled. "And yours?"

"Mr. Goode."

"Is that really your name?" she asked.

"Absolutely." He hesitated. "Do you find that amusing?"

"No...no, not really."

"Well," he continued, "let's dance and get to know each other better."

They talked constantly, while they danced the first set; then the second; and then they started the third.

"Shouldn't we sit this one out?" she asked.

His retort was "Why?"

"Well, I thought..."

"Look, Angel, I want to know you better. Much, much better. Can we get together some night soon?"

"Well, I'm married" she said, "and I don't know when I can get away."

"I'm married too, but certainly we can find some private time to spend alone."

Before she could reply, he said, "How about Wednesday night? Hmm. Let's see where we can meet? I know, how about the Skyward Motel?"

"You're very impertinent" she argued.

"Stop it, Angel, you know you want to."

There was a sly smile on her face. "Wednesday night at 8 p.m." Then she stopped. "What will you tell your wife?"

"Don't worry, I know how to placate her. And you?"

"Not a problem for me. I often go to the movies or shopping alone."

"I'm looking forward to seeing you again. By the way, I have a blue convertible. I can't wait until then."

* * *

It was almost 8 p.m. Wednesday and he had made his way to the Skyward Motel. He chose the back of the motel where there were few cars.

After signing in, he was given the key to a room He waited for Angel. Shortly after 8 p.m. she arrived.

They went into the room together. He thought she was such a sexy lady. He imagined they could have a very good time tonight. His libido was really acting up.

Once in the room, he did not hesitate to pull her into his arms. He kissed her passionately. She responded just as he had hoped she would.

"Angel, you're going to make my night." As they proceeded with the art of seduction and lovemaking, he found himself aroused. Maybe, it was because it all seemed so illicit.

She had the body of an angel, although angels were definitely not as seductive as she was proving to be. What a woman!

In the few hours together, they hit the heights of lovemaking. She enjoyed every moment with him and tempted him endlessly. He, instead, could not get enough of her.

When, at evening's end, they parted, he whispered "How about next Wednesday night? Same time, same place?"

"I'll be here" she replied in her most seductive voice.

* * *

For several Wednesdays thereafter, they met. He thought sex had never been so delicious as it was with Angel. She was encouraged

179

to do many exciting things with him. And he was dying of pleasure and happiness.

* * *

One Wednesday night, as was often the case, they met again. He thought their time together was incredible. She thought he was the most sensuous man she had ever met. As they love-played with each other, he inadvertently scratched her right arm. When that happened, he became very apologetic. "I'm so sorry".

She looked down at her arm. "How will I explain this to my husband?"

"I don't know what to say" he continued. "Tell him you scratched it on your car door."

When they finally departed for the night, he again apologized. He left first. Later, she too drove away.

* * *

When Angel finally arrived home, her husband was waiting for her.

"Where have you been?" he said.

"At the movies."

"Until this hour?" he queried her.

"Lots of traffic" she replied.

When they finally were in bed, he noticed her arm, "What happened to your arm?"

"I scratched it on the car door."

He began to laugh heartily. "Who gave you that lame excuse?"

She stopped short. Then she looked at him directly. "Why you did. When we were at the motel. Don't you remember?"

He hugged her tightly. "I love you, dear wife. You definitely are an angel."

She smiled at him, "Mr. Goode, you are very good at everything you do."

Again she stopped. "Are we going to continue to meet on Wednesday nights at the Skyward Motel?"

"Angel" he said, "we have a great bedroom right here at home. It's all been great fun meeting at the motel. Frankly, although it's been quite exciting for us both to play act, I think for the next few Wednesdays we should stay home. We brought a little spice into our love life, didn't we? I certainly know what you are capable of. As for me wanting you, there is no need to say more about that. I repeat, I love you, my dear wife."

She snuggled close to him and answered, "I love you too, my dear husband."

Home was for eating, sleeping, and lovemaking.

Speaking My Language

SPEAKING MY LANGUAGE

Assandra always had a propensity for languages. She was proficient in Italian and had studied German, Spanish and French. It was of immeasurable help in her European travels. Of course, in some instances she made mistakes, but then those languages were not her native English.

In her work as a travel agent, she had opportunities to visit many countries at a reduced fare. Considering that her work really did not pay well, that was a bonus that more than made up for the lack of monetary remuneration. On occasion there were also "fam trips" whereby an agent traveled free to various countries to become familiar with those countries. This enabled the agent to speak more knowledgeably about travel to those areas to clients.

Reading was also something she enjoyed enormously. Certainly, better than the banal television. With a library close to home, it was easy to spend some time there perusing all sorts of literature and acquainting herself with new and interesting books. She really did not have a preference as to her reading material. Whatever caught her fancy.

The library also held diverse classes for the public. There was a class that reviewed new books; a play time class for children; and a class where English as a second language for newcomers to America was taught. This latter class interested her. She inquired about the requisites for teaching the class. After talking to the head librarian, Cassandra was told she qualified. All she had to do was speak English to the class and help them when they were stymied—sometimes frustrated—with the English language. She was able to explain in their own language the meaning of certain words and phrases idiomatic in English. Each week she received a practice sheet indicating what was to be taught that particular Tuesday. On the first Tuesday night she met the class. She introduced herself to everyone. Among the class members were two Bosnians, a young man from Haiti, one Italian-speaking girl, and several people from Spanish-speaking countries. They were from the Caribbean, Central America and South America. Cassandra—whom some people called Cassie—was somewhat overwhelmed, but she felt she was up to the challenge. It was something she believed she would enjoy.

The class began with the elemental things that people in a new country needed to know. She emphasized the necessity of knowing the English language. All in all, she tried to make it easy and pleasant for all of them. She did not want to see them turn away from the class and not return. Actually, for some people the class was daunting. She reminded them that English was a difficult language. Some languages were relatively simple because each letter in a word was pronounced. How did you tell these people that words like "though, through, and tough" were all pronounced in English.

Because the library was one very large room, Cassie's class was allotted a corner of the room with a large work table where everyone could sit around, along with a blackboard. In front of the library, there was a large check-out desk and a small glassed-in office behind it.

People came and went in the rest of the library, checking out books, making inquiries, or simply spending their time sitting around reading various books or periodicals.

After a couple of weeks, Cassie noticed a dark-haired young man who sat in the corner opposite her class. Usually, he would be reading a book. Now and again, he would look up and spend a period of time observing the language class. Invariably, he would smile. Cassie would return her gaze to her class.

By and large, Cassie's class seemed eager to learn. She did her utmost to help them in their learning pursuit. Some would sometimes get frustrated in trying to absorb this new foreign language, but Cassie was always there to allay their concerns. Repetition of words and phrases often made it easier.

At evening's end she would send the class on its way with homework assignments for the following week's class. The first time she had sent them on their way, she proceeded to pick up her own work books. In her hast,e she dropped a book. The dark-haired man quickly was at her side to help her. She smiled and thanked him. He nodded and smiled in return. As he went out the door, he said, "Bon soir, mademoiselle."

"Merci," she replied. He is probably French, she thought.

Each Tuesday night her enthusiasm for her work grew. She got to know her students better. It was interesting to hear snippets of their lives in their homeland and now in America. They even found time to discuss their aspirations now that they were living in America.

Because of the language problem, many worked in low-paying jobs. Always, however, was the dream of eventually having a better life in America.

The dark-haired man was in his usual spot most Tuesdays, stopping now and again to observe Cassie's class. Sometimes this annoyed her, but she could not do anything. He had a right to be there like all the other patrons.

Somehow he always seemed to leave when Cassie concluded her class. He often held the door for her as she exited the library. One night he said, "Guten abend, fraulein." What, he spoke another language. Having someone speak still another language intrigued her. Who was this man?

Cassie concentrated on her Tuesday class, but she could not help but observe him. He always smiled when she looked at him, nothing more. He seemed to be about her age, but she could not be sure. She wondered why he was always in the library at the same time as her class. Also, what was this man's profession or job? He was always nicely dressed. Lots of questions roamed through Cassie's mind. Very interesting!

Good evening, Cassandra," he said one particular night after her class had concluded.

She was startled. "How do you know my name?" she inquired.

"I noticed it on the blackboard when you begin classes."

She began to stumble over her words. "I... I... I don't know what to say."

He continued, "My name is Henry."

"Pleasure" she said curtly.

He smiled. "I'm not an ogre, you know. I'm here most weeks reading."

"Yes, I noticed" she said. "I'm curious...what do you read?"

"Most anything. Historical books are my preference."

"I see." She moved to leave, but Henry continued speaking.

He added "It's a pleasure to see your enthusiasm when you teach. It seems to transmit to your students, especially when you smile."

Again she stumbled, "...Thank you. Tell me, what is your profession?"

"I buy machinery that makes jewelry. I travel to Europe on many occasions to buy them and then sell them here in the States. I have a smattering of foreign languages." He then hesitated. "Do you have any other questions?"

Haughtily, she answered, "I'm simply making conversation. Remember, you addressed me first."

"You're quite right. Frankly, I wanted to meet you." He stopped and smiled, "Any objection? I didn't mean to make you uncomfortable. You're a lovely woman and I was looking for an opportunity to meet you."

How to end this conversation, she thought. "You'll excuse me. I have to leave now." She couldn't get away fast enough.

As she got in her car, Cassie thought about her awkwardness. She was always comfortable with clients who came to her for travel information. Why was she tongue-tied with this man?

Before she could start her car, she heard a tap on her window. It was Henry. She lowered the window.

"Cassandra, can we go for coffee some place near here right now? You can follow me."

"I... I don't know."

"Cassandra, we are on a very public street with many people about. You are quite safe. Please."

The next thing she knew she was following his car to a nearby coffee shop. They parked adjacent to each other. When she alighted from her car, he smiled and took her hand. Strong hand, she thought.

When they were seated in the coffee shop, he asked what she wanted to drink. "Coffee with cream and sugar, please" she said. He placed his own order also.

She found he was so at ease. She needed to be too.

"You know your name sounds so regal. Are you named after someone special?"

"I'm named after my grandmother."

"Tell me about your work?" he asked.

She proceeded to relate about her work as a travel agent and her language studies.

"You've probably been abroad a few times?"

She nodded.

"Any place in particular that you like?"

"Actually, there are three places, Lake Como, Vienna, Austria, and, of course, Venice."

"I have to agree with you about Venice. Such a unique city. Very romantic. The lack of vehicular traffic there makes it truly special."

They talked about a variety of things. Cassie was now completely at ease. Their coffee cups were refilled as they talked on.

Finally, she said "Henry, I must go. It's been a long day. Thanks for the coffee and the chat." When they arose, she noticed he was not only attractive, but had such piercing eyes.

"Cassandra, this was delightful. I hope we can meet again. Some weeks I'm out of town, but I'd like to see you again. This was a great beginning." He hesitated. "How about Saturday night? Would you enjoy the Philharmonic? I hope you don't have another engagement?"

Only a brief encounter and already he was asking her out. Still, music interested her enormously. Finally, she smiled, "Henry, I would love to attend the Philharmonic."

He arranged to pick her up at 7 p.m. They exchanged addresses and phone numbers. When they separated, he took her hand and kissed it.

As she drove home, Cassie was on Cloud Nine.

That Saturday night they went to the Philharmonic where there was a mixture of classical and pop music. Cassie enjoyed every minute. All sorts of music appealed to her. With music she was in her element.

Henry kept gazing at her. He saw her enthusiasm at the entire program. She would tap her fingers in unison with the orchestra on the arm rests in the theater. "You really enjoyed it all, didn't you?" he said later.

"Oh, yes, I enjoy all types of music, classical, jazz, pop. Overall, music is so soothing to the soul. Thank you for inviting me."

He noticed her eyes glistened. He was entranced by this lovely woman. "There's no better date than the woman I am with tonight." He gave her a brief hug. "How about a nightcap now?"

They drove to a small bar where they had a few drinks and talked further. Then he asked her to dance. She liked the feel of him as he held her. Rather good dancer, she thought. His lips brushed against her temple. So nice, she thought.

At evening's end, he drove her home. "Can we do this again?" he asked. She looked at him and simply replied "Yes." He sweetly kissed her good night and was soon on his way.

Henry called her several times after that. They would go to a movie, a basketball game, a dinner, or just ride around for a bit. They became comfortable with each other. Cassie looked forward to seeing him. Henry never got enough of her.

On the subsequent Tuesday when she convened her class, Henry was not there. She had anticipated his presence, but was disappointed at not seeing him. Perhaps, business, she thought.

Her class was becoming more comfortable in their time together. One night, however, she noticed one of the Spanish girls having difficulty with the current lesson. There was something amiss; something she did not comprehend. She seemed to be crying.

"Anna, tiene usted un problema?" asked Cassie.

Anna did not reply. Suddenly, she arose from her chair, hurriedly put her coat on, and headed for the door.

Cassie ran after her, grasped her arm, and hugged her. "Un momento, Anna." Cassie tried to explain that there would often be problems understanding a new language. Said Cassie, "Ven aqui. Si, el Ingles es dificil." Cassie sat her down and consoled her. Cassie knew this would happen often in these situations. It was harder to teach adults than children. Children absorbed things much easier at a young age. Not so with most adults.

* * *

Cassie had become friendly with the library personnel. Often, they would get together and go someplace for dinner. They were a great group of people and Cassie always enjoyed their company.

An upcoming event was the head librarian's birthday. Together, the library group decided to go to an elegant restaurant to celebrate the occasion. They chose to treat her for her birthday. They all met at a prescribed time on a Friday night. As they entered the restaurant, they were all chatting away. Now they waited for their reserved table.

As they walked to their assigned table, Cassie was somewhat taken aback when she spotted Henry seated with another woman, dining together. The woman was a lovely blond dressed in a very chic outfit. They were very animated in their discussion. He finally noticed Cassie and simply waved. Cassie gulped and waved back. He returned to the lady at hand. Cassie felt awkward. She made it a point to sit with her back to him when her entire group was seated. The conversation among the library people was lively, but Cassie's mind was elsewhere. For Cassie the evening was not turning out as pleasant as she had anticipated. She kept thinking of Henry's presence nearby with another woman.

Finally, Henry and his lady friend left before the library group. Although troubled, Cassie now relaxed and tried to enjoy the rest of the evening with her friends.

When Cassie returned home, she began to mull over who the lady was and what the situation was all about. So much to think about. Did he date others regularly? Questions she should not have been asking herself were roaming through her mind. As a distraction, she sat down to look at the late evening news. Her telephone rang. When she answered, it was Henry.

"Cassie, are you dressed?"

"Yes, but what has that to do with you?"

"Come downstairs. I'm in my car in front of your home."

"Why should I do that at this hour?"

"Cassie, I want to see you now." He emphasized the word "now."

As she often did, she stumbled over her words. "I... I... don't think so."

"Very well, I'm coming in to see you at this moment."

"No, no, no" she insisted. "I'll come out for one minute only."

Cassie put on her shoes and coat. When she was outdoors, he was standing by his car. He looked angry. "Get in the car. I want to talk to you now."

Meekly, Cassie entered the passenger side of his car. Henry started the conversation in an unusual way. "Were you upset when you saw me tonight?"

"Look, I have no right to feel one way or another."

"Tell me about being upset."

"Henry, I repeat I..."

Suddenly he took her in his arms and kissed her over and over. She was stunned.

"Henry, don't do that. You probably just finished kissing one woman and now you're using your charm on me."

"Cassie, just say one thing. Say you cared tonight."

She could not respond because he again began to kiss her.

He repeated, "Say you cared tonight."

She would not let him see the small amount of tears in her eyes.

"Yes, I cared. I have absolutely no right to care about you. We're practically strangers."

"You know as well as I we are never going to be strangers again" he whispered.

"Now, I'll explain. You know that with my business I meet with a number of people from all over who are buying and selling the machines I deal with. It is a very competitive world out there and I have to entertain and be nice with all of them. That elegant lady is in the same business as I. Yes, even women are involved in my business. Do you understand? You may often see me around town with men and women in my business."

She said nothing. She continued to listen to his explanation He smiled at her, "I repeat, do you understand? It's purely business. With you, it's far more than that." Then he finished talking for a moment. Then he quickly resumed. "However, I do want you to repeat what you said earlier. Tell me that you care." He pulled her into his arms. "This is where I want you."

She melted in his arms. "Now go to bed and dream lovely thoughts. I'll pick you up Saturday night and we'll do something together. Is that O.K.?"

He kissed her again and opened the door to let her out.

Several days later she received a call from Henry while at home.

"Cassie, I'm going to Italy on business for about ten days. I'll be leaving Saturday night. I'll try to see you before then, but I'm going to be rather busy. I'll miss you."

"I understand, Henry. Do call me before you leave."

The next day in the travel office she came across some correspondence regarding some Roman hotels that had been refurbished. They were looking for agents to check out the changes they had made. One agent per travel agency would be invited on a free airplane trip. Cassie did so want that assignment. She might be able to see Henry while he was in Italy. She made her pitch to her boss, who said yes and allowed her to represent the agency. The possibility of seeing Henry made her gleeful.

When she called Henry with the news, he was thrilled at the prospect of their meeting abroad. "Henry, since you'll be in the north of Italy, do you think we could meet in one of my favorite cities?"

"I hear Venice," he replied.

"Oh, yes, that would be grand. How about the Hotel Palace in Venice? On the 14th?"

"Perfect. Cassie, do I have to tell you how thrilled at that prospect I am."

All the unexpected travel to be together pleased them both beyond measure.

Henry arrived in Italy on the 10th to conduct his business. By the 14th he would be able to meet Cassie in Venice. He would have a couple of days off. He knew where to contact Cassie in Rome.

On that day, he was at the Hotel Palace in Venice awaiting Cassie's arrival. In the lobby he walked back and forth; then he would sit. The routine was repeated several times before he finally saw her come into the lobby trailing her luggage.

He rushed to greet her. "How's my sweet Cassie" He quickly kissed her.

She caught her breath, smiled at him, and kissed him back.

"Your room is ready. It's on the same floor as mine." He picked up her luggage. "Cassie, go sign in. Maybe you can refresh yourself before we meet. Is that all right? We can meet here in the lobby in about an hour."

Cassie said little but took her carry-on from him and went to her assigned room. After refreshing herself, she changed her clothes and proceeded to meet Henry. She was invigorated at seeing him. Walking hand in hand, he took her to a small cafe for lunch.

Later, they walked up and down the many small bridges that separated each Venetian byway. He never let go of her hand and he never stopped hugging and kissing her. After all, in a romantic city like this it was commonplace to see that sort of behavior.

After a few hours investigating the Venetian byways, they returned to the hotel lobby. They sat there exhausted and just people watched. Then they went to their respective rooms for a little nap.

That evening while waiting for her in the lobby, he saw her come off the elevator beautifully dressed. "Lovely" he said. She wore a simple black dress with colorful costume jewelry and a bright green shawl.

When they arrived in St. Mark's Square, they and all the other people there were feeling the fascination of this unique city and intrigued by all the music emanating from the musicians who were playing for a romantic night. Henry and Cassie looked at each other and smiled broadly. The magic of this city enveloped them.

"Cassie, I think this is the right place to say what I have to say." He stopped and faced her. "I love you, my sweet Cassie."

For this special moment they would both want to remember, she looked at him and said, "Henry, I love you too."

They held each other tightly and could not seem to let go. They were oblivious to everyone around them. This was their special night. Her arms wrapped around his neck while they kissed and kissed again.

Finally, when they let go, Henry said, "There's an elegant restaurant near the Canal where we are going to go for supper. How does that sound?"

"Everything we do together is perfect."

Cassie could not believe the food that was brought them at the chosen restaurant. With each course, there was a different wine. "I'm going to get drunk" she told him. "Cassie, it does not matter. The night is ours."

When they finally arose to leave the restaurant, she turned to the waiter and said, "Ottimo." It meant excellent. The waiter thanked her.

They then went window shopping. The beautiful Murano glass sparkled everywhere in the shop windows. He bought her a small, beautifully colored Murano vase. "What can I get for you?" she asked? He replied, "I have everything I want in you."

It was almost midnight. "How about an aperitif before we call it a night?" "I'll always defer to you" she whispered. Smilingly, he said, "Tomorrow, we take a gondola ride."

They huddled at a small bar, sipping their drinks slowly, and kissing sweetly.

"When you are ready to leave, Cassie, tell me. It's been a long day for you." He noticed her sleepy eyes, "Let's go."

They returned to their hotel, said good night to the desk clerk, and moved on to the elevator. Cassie staggered a little and Henry caught her.

"What a wonderful night in a wonderful city with a wonderful man" she giggled.

"Did you have too much to drink tonight?"

"I don't know and I don't care."

"Let's take the elevator up to our respective rooms, so you can get a good night's rest. It's been quite a night for you, Cassie."

She stepped into the elevator and began humming. Henry looked at her. There was no one else in the elevator. He embraced her and moving her up against the wall, he began kissing her. First, it was sweet. Then it became more passionate. She kept responding by saying "Nice, very nice. I want more."

"You're a glutton for..."

She interrupted, "...kissing."

When they reached their floor, he led her out of the elevator. "Luckily, our rooms are on the same floor."

When she was finally able to get her key in the door lock to her room, she turned to him and said, "Have you seen my room, Henry? It's quite lovely. Come, come."

He stepped into the room, surveyed it completely, and said, "Yes, a great room." Then he stopped and turned to face her, "You should know all these rooms are the same." Then he said, "What's the point of it all, Cassie?"

Before she could reply, he went to the door. "Where are you going?" she asked anxiously.

"I'm locking this door. I don't want any interruptions for what's coming next."

He swept her into his arms before she could say more. "Are you trying to seduce me, Cassie?"

Boldly she turned to him, "I seduce. You produce."

Henry could not help but laugh. "I like your response and I'll do my part."

Before placing her on the bed, he helped her remove her clothing. He was swift with his. When they began to touch each other, the sensual heat was already there. "Cassie, I've been wanting you for so long."

Neither knew how much time elapsed. Actually, there was no need to know. The only need was that which they had for each other. The need had been simmering for some time. His name had never sounded so seductive as when she called him time and time again in the heat of her passion. He was almost senseless with desire for her.

Finally, completely exhausted, he said, "I probably should go to my room."

"Henry, no." She tugged at his arm. "Please stay with me for the rest of the night." She moved in his arms.

"If I do, there's going to be more of the same later. Are you all right with that, my sweet Cassie?" Her eyes said it all. It was going to be a long and perfect night.

After several hours of sleep, they awakened. He said softly, "You were incredible, my sweet Cassie." His lips brushed her forehead.

She sighed, "I almost touched the sky with you."

Before she could say anything further, his mouth sought hers with the same passion he had displayed earlier. All he heard was Cassie whispering his name over and over. All he felt was this seductive wonderful woman in his arms. Once again, he made love to her.

When the morning sun began to flood their room, Henry arose from their bed and turned to Cassie, "Honey, we'll both be leaving Venice in the morning. Shouldn't we do some touristy things today?"

"Very well, Henry." She quickly arose. "I'll take my shower now."

"Cassie, I'm going to my room and take a shower also. I'll get dressed and be back here shortly. Listen, honey, bring a sweater."

After returning from his own room, showered and dressed, he rejoined her. "Okay, let's go, beautiful. Time for some breakfast."

They found a corner bar. They stood up, like the others, and drank an early morning espresso and shared a brioche.

"Now, let's find a gondola and take a romantic ride."

The gondola they chose glided along the waterways of Venice. All the beauty of this unique city filled their senses. Now and again there was some moderate turmoil and uneven motion on the water. Henry then would hug and kiss her, while the gondolier smiled. The man had seen this before.

Once back on land, they headed back to St. Mark's Square. Like many of the other tourists, they fed the pigeons. Cassie grimaced when they fluttered all around her. Not her thing.

"Now let's go to the Cathedral." They found the Byzantine architecture awe-inspiring. "Lovely edifice" he said. Then there was the Doge's Palace, and more.

By noontime they were slowing down. "Should we try a pizza for lunch?" he suggested. "Some place where we can sit for a while."

Cassie agreed to everything he said. Henry was so organized. "Lastly, we should go back to the hotel and rest a bit." Cassie nodded. When they arrived in their room, they flopped on the bed, fully clothed, and had a peaceful siesta.

Towards evening, he said, "Honey, I know I've been organizing everything today, but with so little time I want this to be a special day for us."

"But, Henry, I hope we can do this again."

"Right. However, this evening's program is dinner and dancing."

"Whatever you say," she smiled. Then she added, "Love you."

He placed his arms on her shoulders, "I'm crazy about you." His kiss was very hot and wanting. However, he finally moved away from her. "If this goes on, we'll never leave this room."

Later, when she again alighted from the elevator, while he waited in the lobby, he thought how lucky he was to have her in his life. She wore a pink dress with a small, matching jacket. Her bright smile lit up his heart.

"We're going to another restaurant tonight and fill ourselves up with more Italian goodies. It's no wonder these Italians do so much walking. They have to get rid of all those great calories they ingest."

Cassie was willing to try most foods that were foreign to her. The waiter explained each dish as it was presented. Of course, once again, there was a different wine for each course.

When they left the restaurant, Cassie said, "What a great meal. I am so full I can hardly walk."

"It's just a bit farther to the night club."

The club was small and intimate, but had a great combo playing. It was full of people. When they finally got a table, Henry ordered drinks. The group played some loud music, which made it difficult to talk. Then there was soft smooth music which enabled them to dance. "You love to dance, don't you?" said Henry. She nodded.

With Henry holding her close as they continued to dance, Cassie thought she was in a dream world. Here she was in her favorite city with the man she loved. The proximity of him was absolutely wonderful. She wanted to always relive these moments when their Venetian vacation was over.

When it was almost midnight, they headed back to their hotel. They would not allow themselves to be hurried.

As they got into bed, Cassie prattled on and on about their lovely evening. She told Henry that the dinner was delicious; the dancing was delightful; and their time together was delirious.

"Cassie, all this delicious, delightful and delirious is distracting me from what I have planned for these last moments together." Cassie stopped short and smiled at him. She held her arms open to him. "Hmm" he murmured, "now for a delectable demonstration of my desire for you." Again, he showed her how enamored he was of her.

The next morning they departed Venice, each going his separate way. Henry admonished her about traveling safe. Since he would be visiting various other companies, he told her he would call her when he could after she returned to the States. The final kiss was a long and lingering one.

Several days later Cassie was back at work, filing her report with her boss about her estimation of the various hotels she had visited. Henry called her most nights, despite the time difference. He spoke of his activities during his work day, while she filled him in on hers. He inquired about her language class and she brought him up to date on what had transpired. He was scheduled to return home in about ten days.

Cassie returned to her language class. The students and her library friends inquired about her trip. She did not enumerate what had transpired between her and Henry. She simply said all had gone well.

* * *

When Cassie returned to her Tuesday language class one night, she found most of the students giggling when she appeared.

"What is it?" she inquired.

They continued to giggle; she repeated her question, "What's happened?"

Some pointed to the blackboard. When she turned around, she saw what was written there. In big bold letters it said, "MARRY ME, CASSIE".

She put her hands to her face. "Who did this?" She looked around for Henry, but he was not there.

"Who did this?" she repeated angrily.

She ran to the front desk and asked the librarian, "Who wrote on my blackboard?" She was acting foolishly, but she wanted to put a stop to this.

Turning around, she looked to the front door. In walked Henry with a bouquet of roses. He was smiling broadly. She ran to him. As he managed to hug her with one arm, he said, "Well?"

She could barely say his name and began to cry.

"Cassie, this is not an execution. This is a proposal. After all, we met here."

She held on to him. When she looked at him, she could only say one word. It was a resounding yes.

Then he began with the few foreign words he knew, "Ti amo. Ich liebe dich. Je t'aime." He stopped. "You know what I am saying, sweet Cassie."

Wordlessly, she nodded. Then she began, "Ho capito. Ich verstehe..." She could not say more. He placed the roses on the desk, held her tightly, and kissed her. There would never be a language barrier between them, not at all. How well she knew what he was saying. He was speaking the language of love.

Saturday Matinee

SATURDAY MATINEE

I t started with a kiss. And it ended with a kiss.

The Christmas party at the Carleton Ad Agency was always very festive. The many employees gathered with the higher echelon and laughed and drank away the time. Everything was high quality. The caviar, the champagne, and the elegant hors d'oeuvres. Everyone wore their Christmas finery. Also, they all were on a first name basis. One of Libby's bosses was David.

When all was over, everyone hugged and kissed and happy holiday greetings were exchanged. As Libby prepared to leave, she went to kiss David on the cheek. Instead with open eyes, he kissed her on the mouth. She looked at him. No one had noticed the exchange. She liked the taste. His arm lingered on her shoulder, although he did the same with a couple of other people. When she moved away, she looked at him again. He was staring at her with a half-smile on his face. Then he turned to the next person. Libby hurriedly left the party.

Driving home she went over the events of the party. Strangely, the thought of his mouth on hers had made her feel wanted. It had been a long time since she had been kissed.

David knew nothing of her great unhappiness. When she lost the love of her life, her young son, Matthew, the sadness enveloped her heart and almost strangled the life out of her. She had been a housewife for several years, but her heartbreak forced her to make a decision. She decided to seek some sort of work. It could be a remedy for that which haunted her almost daily.

She readily fit into the work place she had chosen. Getting to know the employees and working and chatting with them on a daily basis brought her some solace. After a couple of years, she had found her groove. She also made some advancement at the agency.

The beauty of her job was her hours. When a project was quickly completed, she, as well as others, could leave early. With a larger project, often most of the employees had to work late into the evening.

One late evening, as the assignments were finalized, David approached both Libby and Peggy, another employee. "C'mon, girls, I'll walk you to your cars. It's pretty dark out there."

As they walked to their cars, David first brought Peggy to her car. "Drive carefully, Peggy. Good night. Thanks for working late." He waved her off.

Next, he walked Libby to her car. "How about a drink before you go on home?" he said casually.

As Libby hesitated, he softly said, "Libby, just a little time together. Meet me at Lester's Pub."

"I have to get home"

"Libby, please."

He got into his car and she got into hers. Lester's Pub was not too far. Maybe, she thought, after a hectic day and night, a drink might be in order. Something brief and quick.

With their cars parked adjacent to each other, he helped her out of her car. They entered the pub together. The place was rather quiet with few patrons. Of course, it was a mid-week night.

When they were seated, he asked her what she wanted to drink.

"You order for me" she said.

"O.K. How about margaritas?"

"Fine" she replied.

They made small talk about the completed project and how the work was going overall.

Then he got more personal. "Where do you live?"

"My husband and I live in Kingston. And you?"

"My family and I live in Highland Estates."

"Must be quite nice" she continued.

"Yes, it's a lovely area" he replied. When he lifted his glass, he said, "To us." Then he stopped for a moment and looked intently at her. "You know when I kissed you at the party, well I really wanted to kiss you again."

Libby looked down and said nothing. Maybe she was anticipating something of this sort.

He took her hand and said, "As you know, I'm a pretty serious fellow, Libby. Being an officer in a large agency consumes a lot of my time and energy." Again, he stopped. "I'm going to say it again now. I want to hold you and kiss you."

Libby moved around in her seat. "David, you've never really looked at me. You are making this so awkward for me."

David returned her pleading look. "Oh, but I have looked. More than you know. However, I have noticed something strange about you. Even when you laugh, there is a sadness in your eyes. Rather unusual."

"I have personal problems" she replied quietly.

"Sorry, I didn't mean to intrude." When he hesitated, he began talking about other things. After they had finished their drink, he said, "I guess if you want to go now, we should." He rose from his seat, paid the tab, took her hand, and led her out the door to her car. "Well, drive carefully going home."

He turned away, but hurriedly turned back to her before she could move. "I said I want to kiss you and..." He pulled her into his arms. He kissed her passionately. Never had she been kissed in that fashion. "Kissing you feels so good. I can't explain it, Libby."

"David," she stammered, "you certainly know how to kiss a woman."

He smiled. "I like hearing that. I am anxious for more. Libby, can we meet sometime? When we have more time?"

As she mulled her reply, he said "All I want to hear is for you to say yes."

"David, what can I possibly say?"

"One word will make me happy, Libby. Say yes".

She was enjoying the feel of him as he continued to hold her It all felt so comfortable. She had not had that in a long time; she needed a man's strength. When she finally looked up at him she said, "Will I be sorry if I say yes?"

"Definitely not." He smiled at her "Go on home and drive carefully. I'll see you at the office. If I arrange for us to meet, you will have to be agreeable." He patted her on the shoulder.

Libby drove away thinking of David's proposition. Yes, there would be no difficulty meeting him. She had a head full of excuses. What could happen with a tryst or two? Maybe she had to feel the presence of a man once more. It was all lacking at home. She and her husband were distances apart since their tragedy. They each were dealing with their sorrow and living their lives separately in their own unorthodox way. Little communication, if at all.

In the office, David strode along greeting every employee. When he reached her desk, he greeted her with a "Good morning. How are you today?" Then before walking away, he whispered "Give me your cell phone number". She hurriedly wrote it on a slip of paper and passed it along to him.

The work day proceeded in the usual way. At the end of the day, her cell phone chirped. "This Saturday afternoon at 1 p.m. at the Hotel Evans. Yes or no?" She replied quietly "Yes" and hung up.

The Hotel Evans was about 25 miles away. She told her husband she would be spending the afternoon at the mall for some browsing and shopping. No questions asked.

As she approached the hotel on Saturday afternoon, she became somewhat apprehensive. Was this right or wrong? Was she that lost and lonely? She was befuddled, but curious about meeting him.

At the hotel she found him sitting in the lobby. Without a word, he rose from his seat. They stepped into the elevator together. Four stories up they stepped out. She followed him to the assigned room.

Once the door closed behind them, all David said was "I'm so glad you came, Libby." Then he smiled at her. "Do you feel uncomfortable?" "Yes and no" she replied.

He tried to put her at ease. He took her hands. "Look at me. All I want is to make love to you. It's as simple as that."

Again, she replied, "I know." Once more, he softly called her name. "Libby, dear Libby."

He sat her on his lap, kissed her, caressed her, and spoke sweetly to her. When he began to undo the buttons on her blouse, she suddenly realized she wanted that. Although it had been a long time, she knew what would follow. She began to unbutton his shirt.

Then she fumbled as she began to unbuckle his belt. He stopped her. "I'll do that."

When they were finally in bed, he said, "I only want you to do one thing now. Place your arms around my neck and kiss me with passion. I'll take care of the rest."

She did as he asked. Suddenly, the wonderful sexual feeling began. He was gentle, but very passionate. He touched her everywhere with such infuriating pleasure. Her murmurs grew louder. Now she found herself participating with greater and greater ardor. "That's what I want" he breathed heavily. It went on and on until the apex drained them both. Finally, they lay side by side without saying anything.

After a while he helped her sit up in bed. "How about something to nibble on." Then he laughingly added "I mean beside you." She agreed.

"I'll call down for some chocolate-covered strawberries and drinks."

"For me, just a soft drink, please" she answered.

He picked up the phone and placed his order. "Won't be long" he added.

When the doorbell rang, he hurriedly put on his trousers and went to pick up the order, while Libby quickly dressed.

They sat next to each other at a nearby table. "Libby, you are a very sexual lady. I can't recall having so much pleasure in a long, long time."

"David, I needed you today," she said without drama. No questions today, he thought. Perhaps another day.

He picked up a strawberry and waited to place it in her open mouth. She savored it. He did it again, while Libby smiled. When he picked up still another, he pulled back his hand and kissed her instead. "You're more delicious than this fruit. Yes, indeed."

As they continued sipping their drinks, they talked about what they knew best. About their workplace and about their lives in general. The hours seemed to hurry by. When she finally rose to leave, he moved the table that stood between them away.

"Libby, no. I don't know when we can meet again. My schedule is sometime hectic, as you know. However, I need to see you. It has to be soon." He held her hands.

He pulled her into the comfort of his arms and said, "Once more, please." Before she could protest, he took her back to bed and again made love to her. She was ready for him. He was as breathless as was she.

As they prepared to leave, all he could say now was "I'll call you, baby." Then one last kiss and David opened the door and closed it behind her. He went to the window of his hotel room and looked down as she prepared to enter her car. He saw her thrust her arms upward in a pleasurable gesture. David smiled broadly, knowing full well he wanted to be with her again.

In the workplace there was not a scintilla of a suggestion as to what had occurred, nor how well they now knew each other. It was all as before. All very business-like.

The second time they met, it was again at the Hotel Evans. However, he had called her on her cell phone late on a Friday night just before all the workers prepared to leave for the weekend.

"I haven't had a chance to call you earlier. A Saturday matinee tomorrow, same place, same time? Are you available?"

Libby replied briefly. "I'll be there."

They repeated the routine of his waiting for her in the hotel's lobby. When they were finally ensconced in their room, he quickly grabbed her. "God, what a week. My looking at you each day. The beautiful scenarios that played in my head. Wanting you. Making love to you. I didn't know what to do and..."

She interrupted him. "David, I'm here." "And I'm happy about that," he replied.

When she was in his arms at last, his entire arsenal of lovemaking came to the fore. She responded in a way that pleased him immeasurably. Finally, he lay back and gave a big sigh. "You're worth waiting for."

Finally, he changed the subject. "I was thinking we could leave here now and..."

"And what?" she queried.

"I know a secluded walking trail near here where we can talk a bit. How does that sound, Libby?" She looked at him, "That's fine."

"I thought we could pick up a coffee and something to eat. We'll use my car. I still have this room for the day, so we can return here."

When they drove away, he picked up some carry-out food. The trail was quiet and secluded. He found a bench for them. "I don't want you to think I have only one thing in mind when I meet you. I want to know more about you and I want you to know about me". Smiling at each other, while enjoying their repast, they talked about many things.

Nothing changed in their respective lives, but there was always the delight of their meeting, being together for a few hours, and sharing some happiness. It was with great anticipation that they looked forward to seeing each other weekly.

Eventually, they began to confide in each other. Outside of what they shared each week, it was the unhappiness that had brought them together.

One Saturday afternoon they had left the hotel and had driven to a secluded trail nearby. The area was interspersed with benches. "Libby, let's sit for a while." She complied. He held her hand. Then David began talking, He started to tell Libby of the plight in his marriage.

"My wife, Felicia, and I were married about eighteen years ago. Like most newlyweds, we were in love. I was doing well in my job and we decided she would stay at home. The hope was that we could immediately start a family. When we finally had our twin boys, I was over the moon. They were beautiful and healthy. However, Felicia began losing interest in the intimacy we had. Now she felt that was for procreation only. Besides, in reality, it was difficult taking care of two boys. Her change of heart came rather rapidly. The physical aspect between us was important to me. I explained that to her, but it all fell on deaf ears. She would not go to counseling. She was adamant in her decision. My boys were very important to me. They were my joy.

"I was utterly shaken. I was like a stranger in my own house. All I did was provide for all four of us. I began to golf more frequently. I even took up tennis. I had to do anything to keep my sanity and stay occupied. Frankly, hard to believe, but I even lost interest in women. Really, I was just a solitary figure. Everyone around us did not know that. We seemed to be a happy family. So the facade began."

His head went down and he placed his head in his hands. Libby took his hands and caressed them. When he looked up, he smiled at her. "Then you came along. I saw a sadness in your eyes, but I didn't want to take advantage of that. However, I kept thinking of you and seeing you every day, well that did something to me. Despite the consequences, I suddenly knew I wanted to know you better. The difference was that as we got to know each other and spent time together, something happened. Libby, I fell in love with you."

He placed his arms around her, awaiting her reaction. Libby said nothing, but simply smiled at him. For several moments, all they did was hold each other. Nothing more was said.

One particular Saturday David waited for Libby to arrive. It was getting late. She might not be coming, he thought. He paced back and forth in the hotel room. Now and then, he looked out the hotel window looking for her car, but to no avail. There was no response when he dialed her cell phone. He tried it more than once.

After almost an hour, there was a knock on the door. He hurried to open it. It was Libby. She could see the anger in his face and hear it in his voice. "Where have you been all this time? Tell me where?" He pulled her into the room.

Libby stared back at him. "You have no right to talk to me that way."

"I had no idea what happened and where you were" he said loudly.

"Well, there is an air show near here and the traffic is horrendous."

"Why didn't you call me," he argued.

"You may have my cell, but I don't have yours. How was I going to manage that?" she replied smugly. She turned and walked away from him.

He grabbed her arm. "Don't walk away from me."

She raised her voice, faced him and said, "I'm not your chattel."

"No, but I'm the guy who loves you most of all."

She stopped in her tracks. When he went to her, he repeated, "You heard what I said. I love you, Libby."

Libby lay her head on his chest. "Yes, I heard."

All the anger dissipated when he said, "Libby, my Libby."

For several minutes he held her. "Our time together is short; every moment means a lot to me. We have our screwed-up lives to deal with." He caressed her face. "I want our time together to be special." He continued holding her. She said nothing. There was only the warmth of his embrace.

Most of their Saturday matinees were at the Hotel Evans. When they met they made it a point to catch up on all that had transpired during the week—those moments when they were not in the work place interacting with the other employees. At work it was all business. They doubted that anyone suspected what was occurring between them. Libby often said that their time together was precious. David agreed. Those few hours they were relaxed with one another and told each other everything. To share completely was what they needed.

One Saturday when they met she looked especially sad. "Do you want to talk?" David asked.

"Not right now. I just want to sit for a bit." She sat on the sofa that faced out where there was a little creek and some trees. David said nothing; he did not want to disturb her thoughts. When she was ready, she would talk to him.

"Here, I'll hang up your coat" he said. When he turned away to do that, she began to sob. He hurried over to her. "Baby, what's the matter?" Her sobs grew louder. "He hugged her tightly. "Baby, it's all right."

Loudly she cried out, "No, no. It will never be all right. Not ever. My baby is gone. I'll never see him again."

Then David knew. She was overcome by thoughts of her lost child. She cried and cried copious tears. He did not know what to say. All he could do was hold on to her. "God, I don't know what to say, Libby. I love you. I don't want to see you punishing yourself like this."

"Do you know what happened, David? Do you know?" He shook his head.

"My little boy had a terrible pain in his leg. When we took him to Emergency, they did not know what was the matter. Eventually, they found a bacteria had invaded his entire body. In three days he was gone. My baby."

David was at a loss for words. The grief was still palpable to her.

He picked her up and placed her on the bed. After some time her tears subsided. All he could do now was sit by her side and touch her now and again.

He sat her down. "Baby, shall I order some drinks?"

"Something very strong" she said.

He smiled. "I think not. You have to drive home later."

David picked up the phone. "Send up a chilled bottle of champagne and two glasses."

Waiting for the champagne to arrive, he said, "I'm sorry I never gave you my cell phone number." He wrote it on a slip of paper and gave it to her. "Don't lose it."

David continued to look at her. "Have you had a good week?" She smiled and nodded. Then David laughed. "If we have nothing to talk about, what are we doing here?" Then he went on, "As they do in the movies, he swept her off her feet." Quickly, he picked her up in his arms. "It's bed time." Libby again smiled as she placed her arms around his neck.

It all proved to be so romantic. What lovemaking should be. "Yes," he whispered, "you're what I want and need."

Libby did not respond, but as her murmurs grew louder, David knew how satisfied they both were.

* * *

In the workplace they were always cordial, but reserved. When no one noticed, they would look at each other and give a loving smile. Some days were harried, as such things were; other days were more tranquil. Libby would often lunch with one or two of the office employees. She had a good rapport with them. When much later David called Libby, he said, "I'm going to New York City for the weekend for a brief meeting. However, I definitely have time for you there. What do you think?"

Libby thought and thought about his suggestion. "I could see one of the plays for a matinee."

"Love the way you think, baby. Let's work out the details. It's just a two-hour train ride."

When they had finalized their plans, Libby simply told her husband she was going to New York City to see a matinee for a popular play there. As always, there was no response or argument. He was invariably taken with his own thoughts and simply said little. Libby said no more.

The Yorker Hotel was their meeting place. David had arrived beforehand and sat waiting for her arrival. All he could say when he saw her was, "Hi, baby. Want to do lunch first?" She agreed.

While walking to an eatery, David stopped. Fortunately, they were not holding hands. Coming towards them was his neighbor, Jane. Quickly, David took the bull by the horns. Libby was truly startled.

"Hey, Jane, surprising to see you here. What are you up to?"

Jane looked askance at both of them. Hurriedly, David said, "Why my colleague Libby here and I are catching up with those other colleagues up front for lunch." He pointed up ahead to a group of people walking. He did not know the people from a hole in the wall, but he had to say something. Smiling at her, he said, "We had a business conference this morning, so now it's lunch time." He continued talking to Jane, while Jane looked from one to the other. Then he said, "What a small world. So, what are you doing here?" He was thinking he had to put the ball in her court now.

Jane was more at ease now that she had heard his explanation. "I'm meeting some friends for shopping. Nothing like the beautiful things you can find in New York City."

"That's true." said David "Well, you'll excuse us but we have to catch up with our friends before we lose them. See you later."

He hastened his walk. "Don't say anything, baby. I'll explain."

Everything had happened so rapidly that Libby truly did not know what to say.

"Baby, she's my neighbor. I had to have it all look kosher. You understand now when I say let me do the talking." Sarcastically, he added, "One lie begets another."

Libby was digesting it all. She said nothing for the rest of their walk to the restaurant.

As they took their seats in the restaurant, he took her hand. "Libby, don't get upset. We'll talk about it later. Okay?"

"Yes, David, but I'm upset this moment. However, as you said, we'll talk later."

David looked at the menu. "You know the lobster and salmon are great here. Do you have a choice?"

"I'll have what you have" she said. "Plus an iced tea."

He digressed. "Did I tell you how beautiful you are and how I love being alone with you?"

Libby arched her eyebrows. "David, I won't spoil our day."

They had a leisurely lunch and then walked back to the Yorker Hotel. He went to the front desk and asked for his key. Soon they were settled in their hotel room.

After he kissed her for just a moment, he said somewhat angrily, "Look, we are not going to go to a monastery to see each other. If I had a choice, I would show you off to the entire world. I'm going to continue seeing you as much as possible. I want you more than you know. Do you understand?" "And" he continued "we are here because I am planning to make love to you." David approached her.

What could Libby say. She was here for the same reasons as David.

Their afternoon together was blissful. "It gets better all the time" he whispered. Libby would not let anything bother her. She was where she wanted to be. His arms encompassed her.

She took an early night train home. David said he would wait for the next one.

* * *

The plane had arrived on time. Libby waited at curbside for David. He said he would pick her up in a white rental. He was prompt. He jumped out of the car, gave her a peck on the cheek, placed her luggage in the trunk, opened the passenger side of the auto, kissed her again, and said, "Hi, baby. So happy to see you." She kissed him back.

Once ensconced in the car, she heaved a big sigh. "Do you have lots to tell me?"

"Those darn conventions are so boring by and large. Those three days seemed like forever." He stopped and looked at her, "Did everything go well when you left home?" She nodded. Many things were best left unsaid. "It's a short ride to the Pink Palace. I think you'll enjoy it."

The Florida air, sunshine, and breezes were so soothing. Libby just sat back, closed her eyes, and said nothing more.

When they finally arrived, she gazed at the hotel and said, "What a lovely place. I know this hotel is world renowned."

Their room was at the back side of the hotel, facing the waters. When David opened the double doors to their room, she surveyed the entire room and ogled it all, saying, "How gorgeous."

He swung her around to face him. "That's what I always say when I see you. How gorgeous."

Everything became more beautiful when his deep kiss took her by surprise.

With her arms around his neck she said, "If it was a log cabin, I might have said the same thing."

David smiled at her. "Well, that probably will be our next adventure." He picked her up and whirled her around. "Now, listen, baby. Do you want to go bathing in the hotel pool or the ocean?"

"The pool sounds nice," she replied.

"Well, let's put on our bathing suits and get going. We're wasting time."

As Libby sought her swim suit in her luggage, she noticed, however, that suddenly he had stopped.

"David, what's the matter?"

He quickly approached her. "I told you we're wasting time. I haven't seen you in days and I want to test the bed first. If we have complaints about that, we can let the management know. What do you think?" He was caressing both her arms.

Libby stopped and began to laugh. "You're sly, David. You're sly."

He picked her up in his arms and headed for the bed. "Let's do some testing. I'll have to check your entire body to see if everything fits well."

Again, Libby laughed as she held on to him. She was crazy about this man. He brought her joy.

Much later he turned to her and said, "Shall we complain to the management?"

"You know what I'm going to say." She emphasized "No."

"Seriously, Libby, I think we should get dressed for dinner now. They have first-class chefs and cuisine here. Let's go check it out."

After David had dressed, he sat leafing through a magazine while Libby was preparing herself in the dressing room. When she emerged, he stood up. All he said was "Gorgeous."

She was dressed in a white off-the-shoulder blouse, along with white silk slacks."

"Am I your date for tonight?" he said.

"Absolutely."

"By the way, baby, I want to tell you that wherever we go, we can easily run into people you or I are apt to know. You are not to get flustered. In most cases, I'll handle things. Do you agree?"

"Whatever you say."

The following day, he said, "Come on, baby, let's take a walk by the beach. No shoes or socks. Just the refreshing feel of the water on our feet. This is a lovely spot. What do you think?" Libby nodded in agreement. As they walked along the water's edge, they held hands. The Florida day was ideal. Blue sky, blue water, warm breezes, people vacationing and enjoying it all.

"You know, Libby, why is it that two unhappy people like you and me should find happiness together?"

"I don't know, David. I only know whatever it is feels wonderful to me. I'm never in the doldrums when I'm with you."

He held her even closer. "You're the best medicine for me. Now that I've found you, I'll do anything to keep you." His sweet kiss on her forehead reassured her. They walked the entire length of the beach and then back again. Sometime saying nothing and simply enjoying it all was what they needed.

Other times they would take advantage of the hotel's many amenities. The massages at the hotel's spa were so soothing. The exercise room, with its various machines, was invigorating. After sweating away for a time, they returned to their room, showered and rested in each other's arms. Nothing more.

David even insisted she try playing tennis with him. "But, David, I've never played before." He showed her how to hold the racquet and ball. When he lobbed the ball, she could not retrieve it and got frustrated. "Baby, forget it. It's only a game. No trophies to win." As they both approached the net, he added "You're my trophy."

When they were at poolside another day, he asked if she knew how to swim. She said yes. The hotel pool was large and shaped like a sea shell. When David saw her climb up to the diving board, he was astonished. She made a beautiful swan-like dive into the water and swam the length of the pool. When she emerged, she strutted before him. "Well?" she said.

"Libby, you always surprise me. You're great. I owe you a kiss."

When she smiled at him, all he could think of was not only how crazy he was about her, but also how her sadness had flown away for a little while.

Later David mentioned his plans for the night. Enjoying every moment in their limited time together was what he wanted for both of them. Also, he could see that any diversion relaxed her.

There was a restaurant a couple of miles away that was unique. It was called L'Artiste. It contained several paintings by well-known artists. It was part small museum and part elegant restaurant.

"I've made reservations for 8 p.m. What do you think?" Invariably, Libby agreed. For this occasion she wore a simple black dress, cut low in front, with a large faux rose at the bodice. "Black is sexy," he smiled.

They drove the two miles to the restaurant. Libby marveled at how exquisite everything was. The paintings they perused were so lovely. The entire meal was extraordinary. They lingered after dinner and had a post-prandial on the lanai of the restaurant. At the end of the evening she simply said, "Perfect evening."

When they returned to their hotel room, he said, "Well, this is our last night together." She put her finger to his lips. "Just for now, dear David. Just for now."

"Libby, I don't want to pry, but how were you able to get away from home for this length of time?"

She could not lie to David. She was leading an upside-down life. "I said I was going to visit my cousin in Florida. No questions asked."

"Look, I don't want to make life difficult for you, but you know I always want you close to me, even if I don't have that right." He caressed her cheek.

"David, these last years there have been virtually no questions asked about our individual movements. We live in the same house, but, like you, we simply present a facade to others. For now, don't be concerned."

"Oh, but, baby, I am concerned. I truly am." Wrapping their arms tightly around each other now was keeping the rest of the world at bay.

* * *

Libby was doing some gardening at the front of her home. It was something that had always given her pleasure.

She heard a car stop in front of her home. A woman alighted and approached her.

"Are you Libby."

"Yes. What can I do for you?"

"I am David's wife, Felicia. You can guess why I am here."

Libby anticipated an unpleasant situation. "I think you better come in. I don't want the neighbors to hear what you have to say."

When Felicia entered the home, she also confronted Libby's husband, Frank.

"No sense in beating around the bush. You've been seeing my husband for some time."

"Well, we do work together" said Libby. What else could she say.

"Oh, come now. You've been having an affair with David. You meet outside of work, don't you?"

Frank looked at them both. "What is she talking about, Libby?"

There was a knock on the front door. When Libby opened it, she saw David. God, what a conundrum this was going to be.

David faced his wife, "What are you doing here, Felicia?"

"Let's stop playing games here everyone." She turned to Frank. "Did you know?"

Frank was completely dumbfounded. If anyone was in the dark, it was Frank.

Angrily, Felicia continued, "You have broken up my home, Libby. You have brought much upheaval to a loving family."

"Felicia, stop lying. We haven't been a loving family for some time. Don't try fooling any one."

"We have two young boys. That must mean something to you, David."

"Yes, they absolutely do. More than you know. However, they are going off to college in the fall, so they are adults. Besides, you have no right to come here and confront these people without venting your spleen on me first. I could have talked to you privately. Why this?"

"I've been humiliated by what has been going on between you two."

Then Frank interjected. "This is our home. Libby and I have undergone a great sorrow without my having to hear this." Frank's face was ashen.

Felicia turned to Frank. "How you handle things is your business. I won't have this disruption in my family."

"Felicia, you've done enough damage today" said David.

Before more could be said, Frank looked at each of them. "Libby has had to deal with a dreadful tragedy. I forgive her for whatever she did." Frank looked at Libby.

"I forgive you, Libby." Suddenly, he realized something was amiss; something terrible was happening to their lives.

Libby was speechless at the course of these events. Then she got angry at them all. "You don't know anything about the utter sadness I've endured." She screamed, "Get out of my life all of you."

In other circumstances, David would have pulled her to him. Now he was paralyzed. He too did not want to lose her.

"As for you, David, you will pay for this. Playtime with your employee will cost you," said Felicia.

David's retort was, "If whatever happened was right or wrong, you will not threaten me, Felicia."

After what seemed an interminable time, they dispersed. Felicia was the first to storm out the door. Once more, she made threats as to what she was planning on doing to get back at David.

Next it was David. He looked at Libby for some sort of a response. She looked back, but said nothing. He was despondent. He slowly walked out the door to his car. He had lost her.

Frank's eyes locked onto Libby's. Libby seemed to be perplexed and in a state of confusion, but she had to say something to Frank. She owed him that much. She touched his arm. "Frank, thank you for your act of forgiveness, but there will always be pain between us. We've been unable to pull together after our great loss. I can't stay... I can't." She couldn't tell him more. She kissed him on the cheek. She ran to her room, picked up her jacket and purse, and ran out the door.

Frank was desolate. He lowered his head to the table. What had been dear to him was now gone. Without consideration or compassion for each other, everything between them had been destroyed. After all these years, all was lost. He began to sob uncontrollably. This would be what he had to bear forever.

Libby rushed out the door. "David, David, wait for me. Please." Her feet couldn't move fast enough. David heard her voice. He stopped his car and looked back. He opened the passenger door, grabbed her arm and pulled her into the car. "Libby, Libby, I love you.

I want you forever," he cried out. He had the biggest smile on his face.

"David, there's a walking trail near here where we can talk" she said breathlessly, as she now sat next to him. His right hand held hers tightly. When they finally arrived at the trail, they found a bench and began talking rapidly, both at the same time.

"Baby, there's always someone who gets hurt in these situations. I didn't want to see anyone hurt. Our past may always haunt us. I don't know what will happen. There's a lot we have to sort out. I just know what I want from now on." He held her close and kissed her over and over.

"Please" she said, "there is so much we must talk about." "Libby, my love," he reassured her "everything will be all right." He was beaming. They kissed continually.

Two young men walking by looked at them and shook their heads. "Why don't you two get a room."

About the Author

Marianne Borgia has lived in Rhode Island her entire life. After a lengthy marriage, she decided to pursue writing after her husband's death. It prompted her to think of the many love stories that are never told. Her own love story is most interesting, bur for now she has chosen to write about others. Her soul is soothed by a good book and all types of music.

www.ingramcontent.com/pod-product-compliance
Lightning Source LLC
Chambersburg PA
CBHW070730280626
47159CB00023B/3038